three *by* three

ben fletcher
three *by* three

All The Best,

BFletch

First published internationally in 2016 by Blue Lens
Blue Lens is an imprint of Blue Lens Films Limited

A CIP catalogue record for this book is available from the British Library

ISBN   978 0 9935 5151 2
            3 5 7 9 8 6 4 2

Blue Lens Films Limited, registered in England and Wales at
71-75 Shelton Street, Covent Garden, London, WC2H 9JQ

bensfletcher.com

International Edition
Printer and binder may vary between territories of production and sale

for Hannah

contents

chapter one
the estate

The industrial estate on the edge of town had, for a number of years, not been a place that attracted all that many people.

Not many of the right sort of people anyway.

The forest of old brick buildings that once stood clean and tall were now covered in several thick layers of moss, while the accompanying metal plated factories that were once able to reflect the sun's rays for miles into the distance were now a dull, dirty grey and starting to show noticeable signs of rust.

The entire estate had, at one time, been owned by a single very large and very successful business that'd employed thousands of people from the local area.

Campbell Urwin Limited had been one of the countries largest manufacturing companies. It produced everything from branded food for supermarkets to small and complicated

three *by* three

plastic components for computers.

Everything changed, however, when eighteen years earlier a recession hit the economy and the companies founder and owner, a man who'd always been an honest, hard-working philanthropist and highly regarded member of the community, began to face increasing stress and financial pressure.

It was early one Friday morning, a few days after the company had lost over half of its value overnight, that his car was found by a police officer parked just a short distance away from a large bridge that provided passage over the deep and fast moving river that ran below it.

In the weeks that followed the production lines began to slow before eventually, they came to a stop altogether. After that, the entire estate was left to fall into disarray.

Ever since then, the only people who ever made a visit to the area were estate agents attempting to win the office award for the most unlikely sale of the year and groups of school children messing around at the weekends or during the holidays.

They were the only innocent visitors anyway.

The out of town location and little policing of the area had made the estate a haven for a broad scope of criminal organisations (and some not so organised criminals too). Many of them did little more than offer drugs or prostitution to anyone who was desperate enough to travel out.

the estate

Over time, the estate had also come to be the home of a group who's time was focussed on much more sinister actives. They were a group of people who went by no formal name and a group whose presence there was unknown to all those who passed through the area.

The group called home a building that stood in the middle of the vast estate. It was a building quite different from those that surrounded it. It was cleaner (although not by much), as well as taller and much more modern than the rest. It had, formally, also been the head office of Campbell Urwin.

The top floor of the building was made up of a number of small rooms. They'd all previously been the offices of the company's top executives, although none had been used to house office equipment for some time. More recently the rooms had been converted and become improvised bedrooms.

In the far corner of the floor was a small and fairly basic room with little in it apart from a rusty bed frame topped with a mattress so old it was made up of considerably more broken springs than not.

This particular room belonged to the girl that was sat on the splintering chair by the window and looking out at the view, although there was little she was able to see through the heavy torrent of rain and hail that was smashing its way down onto the glass.

Cleo was an average girl of average height. In fact, almost everything about her was average, apart from her life anyway,

three *by* three

that was nothing near average.

She often spent much of her time looking out of this window. So much so that she'd gotten to recognise the faces of many of the estate's regular visitors quite well.

Every Friday evening, without fail, there was an old man who'd arrive just before seven to pick up his regular girl from the corner of the next street before returning several hours later to drop her off again, often with a much different facial expression.

On Monday's there was usually a fight between the various rival groups of drug dealers at they battled for customers. Cleo had never been able to work out why this only ever seemed to happen on Monday's. The best reason she could think of was that many businesspeople often found illegal narcotics to be their only way of making it through the remainder of the week.

Soon after dusk fell on Wednesday nights, there was even a regular group of couples who'd meet up and park in a circle before admiring the interiors of each other's cars one by one... or at least that was what Cleo preferred to think they were doing anyway.

It wasn't that Cleo didn't want to live an average life, in fact, it was the only thing she ever had wanted. It was that her family would never have approved of her having such a life.

When she was only a few weeks old, she was left in care by her parents. There was little she knew about why they left her

4

the estate

or even who they were: they'd never once come back to visit her, not even at Christmas or on her Birthday. There had been many times she considered trying to find them herself, but she'd always had little idea of where to start.

As she grew up, she'd been welcomed in by a number of families, although she'd never stayed with any of them for longer than just a few months. Not feeling as though they were ready to commit to bringing up a child was often the reason they gave as they returned her to care, but Cleo had always known that the real reason was because she simply found it difficult to trust of bond with anyone, even if they only ever had her best interests in mind.

She'd found her teenage years to be even harder. Being in care meant that she only ever had the very basic of everything, and as such, she'd never been able to fit in with the crowd during her time at secondary school. Not once did she ever receive an invite to one of the in crowd parties that one of the more popular girls would host, and as for receiving any interest from the males... the only time she ever got any attention from them was if they were going out of their way to push past her in the corridor or trying to win a bet they'd made at one of the many parties she wasn't invited to.

She left school shortly after her seventeenth birthday. Not that anyone, even the school, ever noticed her suddenly stop turning up one day.

It was soon after that when she found her new family.

5

three *by* three

They weren't necessarily a family in the traditional sense as such, but they were the closest she'd ever had to one. Family was also what they proffered her to consider them as and she knew that it was always a lot easier (and safer) to go along with what they wanted.

As she continued to watch the patterns forming from the water running down the glass in front of her, she reached under her shirt to grasp in her hand the small pendant of the necklace she was wearing.

The necklace was the only thing her parents had left her with and one of the only things she'd ever owned herself. It was something that she valued above anything and everything else.

Held securely within the pendant there was a single small gemstone that shone brightly even in the smallest amount of light. It was a stone that at a quick glance could quite easily be mistaken for a diamond, even by those with a trained eye. Cleo, however, had always someone known it wasn't a diamond, there was something different about it, not that she'd ever seen an actual diamond herself to compare it with.

She often spent time holding the pendant. She also often thought about where her parents were and who they actually were. A lot of the time she also found it difficult not to wonder if they ever thought the same about her.

Other than the continuous thudding created as the rain hit both the window and roof above her, there was little else that

the estate

could be heard until, all of a sudden, the thudding began being drowned out by a much louder banging sound coming from the room below.

Although at first she couldn't help but flinch at the suddenness of it, she was mostly accustomed to such loud noises. The walls and floors within the building were all quite thin, and the occupants within them weren't often the quietest of people.

Cleo was often excluded from family discussions, even those that were about her, but she'd come to learn that it was possible to hear almost everything that was being said simply by placing her ear to the floorboards, after all, there was very little else separating her from the room below anyway.

And so, as she heard what sounded like the start of another conversation that she wasn't to be a part of she placed the necklace back under her shirt and moved to the floor to press her ear up against the damp wooden boards.

She was able to hear the voices of three men, although only one that she was able to recognise, the voice of Ivan, one of the people she lived with. As for the other two, she'd never heard either of them before.

'Isn't it risky for both of you to be coming here?' she heard Ivan ask the other two men, although, from the tone of his voice, she couldn't help but think that he sounded more concerned about himself rather than either of them.

'If anyone is watching this place then we'll be sure to know

7

about it… he's keeping an eye on that for us after all,' replied one of the other two men. Although she wasn't sure who he was talking about, she could only presume that it was the third man who was yet to speak.

'I have been, and I continue to as much as I can,' began the third man. 'But you must understand, it's becoming harder, I don't want to draw any suspicions.'

'I do hope you haven't forgotten your place in all of this,' replied the second in a slow and icy voice.

'I'm inside,' replied the third, almost nervously so.

'You were inside before all of this. You've done well to get yourself in the position you're though. Of course, there will soon be much more for you to do.'

Cleo wasn't sure what they were talking about, but this was often the way she found it to be. Her family had always liked to keep secrets from her.

In an attempt to try to make some sense from what she kept overheard, she'd started a journal to write things down in. And so like she'd before, she lifted her ear from the floor and reached under her bed to retrieve a small and tatty looking leather bound book along with a near blunt pencil.

'Is it safe for us to be taking the next step yet?' she heard the second man continue as she placed her ear back to the floor.

'Nearly,' replied the third. 'Most of them are too busy investigating the plane crash.'

the estate

'And I presume you've already made sure that there will be no inconvenient suspicions about that?'

'None. I've made sure of it. They'll blame the girl.'

'And what about you Ivan?'

'She's nearly ready,' Ivan replied after a longer than comfortable pause.

'Are you sure she'll be the right person for this?' interrupted the third man. 'She's only a girl after all.'

'Well if for any reason she turns out not to be the right person then I'm sure Ivan will be more than aware of the inconvenience it'll cause to his own personal well-being.'

'I need to make sure,' Ivan began. 'She'll be the only one who's blamed for any of this won't she?'

'I wouldn't worry about that. Every good plan needs a goat and she's ours. She'll take the blame for whatever we need her to.'

'I still don't understand why you're going this far.' By now Ivan was starting to sound irritated with his visitors.

'Because it's time someone else suffered.' A short pause followed. 'You aren't having any second thoughts are you Ivan?'

Ivan didn't get a chance to respond. Instead, the conversation was interrupted by a phone ringing out from the pocket of one of the three men.

'I need to go,' said the third man.

'It's probably time I went too,' replied the second. 'I expect

three *by* three

you to make sure she's ready by the end of next week Ivan. We've waited long enough now.'

Cleo continued to listen but after a short time she heard the sound of a door slam shut, and she knew the two men had left.

Curious to see who they both were, she quickly stood up and went over to the window.

Although the water running down the glass made it impossible to see anything clearly, she was just about able to make out the outlines of the two men as they walked towards what looked like the broad outlines of two cars parked on the nearby road.

To give herself a better view she tried to open the window but at first, her attempts were hopeless. Years of neglect had meant the metal frame had become stiff and glued shut with rust. She tried again, and again before eventually as she tried one final time it swung open with a loud clang and a swift damp breeze began filling the room.

From so high up it wasn't possible for her to make out any distinguishing features of either of the men, although she reckoned that they must've been in their late twenties or early thirties. There was one thing she knew for sure though, she'd never seen either of them before.

She waited and watched them drive off around the corner before turning her attention back to her journal. She only had the chance to write a single word before there was another loud and sudden bang, although this time it was from just outside her room. Again she wasn't so shocked. In fact, she was almost expecting it, after all, this bang meant she was about to receive a visit from what sounded like a very angry and very irritated Ivan.

Ivan often came to see her whenever he was feeling angry or irritated, although it wasn't necessarily so he could receive comfort or moral support. He'd his own, rather unique ways to make himself feel better whenever he was angry, and often they were ways that involved Cleo sustaining a new injury of some sort.

She knew she only had a few seconds before he'd walk in and so, in a panic, she threw her notebook under her bed and out of sight, followed shortly afterwards by the necklace. Ivan knew about neither of them and that was very much the way she wanted to keep it. Not wanting him to suspect that she'd been listening in on his conversation she also sat back down on the chair by the window.

Moments later there was another loud bang from the other side of the door as Ivan kicked it open. It was followed almost instantly by a sharp crack of splitting wood as it swung round on its rusty hinges and hit the wall behind.

She looked up to face the tall and muscular man that was now stood in her doorframe with nothing but a clear look of frustration upon his rough and unshaven face.

It came as a surprise to Cleo when he then took a step towards her as though he wanted to give her a hug. As he got

three *by* three

closer however, it wasn't long before he resorted to type. He grabbed her by the arm and using all his strength he threw her straight out of the room and into the opposite wall of the outside corridor.

She hit the wall with such a loud thud that anyone who happened to be sleeping in any of the other nearby rooms would almost certainly have been woken up. Or at least they'd have been if they'd not become used to having such noises accompanying their own dreams every night.

If there was only one thing that was dirtier than any of the rooms it was the dark and dingy corridor that connected them. It was a place that was fast becoming a museum of cobwebs and somewhere that'd clearly not been cleaned for some years.

'You should be working harder this week,' came Ivan's voice through the dust cloud that'd appeared as she hit the wall.

'I'm trying,' she coughed as she pulled herself back up from the floor.

'Well, I need you to be trying much harder.'

As the dust settled, she looked down the corridor towards the staircase that led to the floor below. She knew that if she wasn't able to reach it before Ivan, then she'd likely be thrown down it.

She managed to make it to the bottom of the staircase just in time. But following briskly behind and giving her no chance to catch her breath, Ivan then grabbed her by the collar and pushed her up against the wall.

'It…' she began, unable to talk clearly. 'It isn't so easy,' she continued. 'Ever since…'

'Ever since what?' he interrupted, tightening his grip.

'Ever since you killed that man.'

He released his grip and watched as she fell helplessly onto the floor in front of him. Cleo tried to pull herself up but he didn't give her a chance. Instead, he pushed her back down again, this time in front of a nearby door.

Ignoring her struggle for breath he then stepped over her and walked casually through the door.

Eventually, once she'd picked herself up again, she followed, limping into the room.

Atop a table in the corner of the room was a broad and varied selection of weapons, many of which held answers to most of the towns rapidly increasing number of violent crimes.

Cleo looked at Ivan but he was too focused on the table to notice she'd followed him into the room. She watched as he picked up an axe from the table top and began gently brushing his finger along its edge.

'What are you trying to get me ready for?' she asked, knowing immediately it was a mistake to do so.

Ivan turned and walked up towards her in a rage, still holding the axe in his hand.

'I really don't think that you should be listening in on any of my conversations,' he said in an icy tone as he used his free hand to push her up against the wall. 'Nor do I care for any excuses you have.'

There was little Cleo could do as she watched him push the blade of the axe through the fabric of her sleeve and then into the wall behind, trapping her where she was.

'I would suggest that you don't either,' he continued, now whispering slowly into her ear. 'It would be a great shame if it were to become ever harder because someone else had to take their final breath this evening wouldn't it.' With that he turned and walked out of the room, leaving her stuck where she was.

Cleo waited for a short while to be sure that he wasn't coming back and then, as she looked down at the axe holding her in place, a thought flooded her mind. She could use it there and then to attack Ivan, the opportunity was there for her. He'd never expect it coming. But then she knew she'd get caught. Other people lived within those walls and they'd be sure to hear anything that happened. Besides, even if she wasn't caught, she didn't have anywhere to go afterwards.

She took a deep breath and pulled the axe out of what was now a large dent in the wall. Holding it firmly in her hand she knew what she needed to do and she knew she had no choice about it.

chapter two
friday night

For many that evening marked the end of what had been a very long week at work.

It was the second Friday of the year, and that meant the majority of people had just spent the previous five days working much longer hours than usual in a frenzied attempt to catch up with their ever growing to-do lists that'd built up during their Christmas break.

Despite the torrential rains and noticeable January chill in the air, the atmosphere around the towns brand new multi-million-pound leisure park was one full of cheerful thoughts and excitement as people gathered to spend the evening relaxing with their friends and family, whatever the weather.

Grouped up around the park friends huddled together. Many people had badly misjudged the weather while getting ready earlier in the evening and had, by now, resorted to attempting to convince the one person who'd remembered to bring an umbrella that they'd always been their favourite person in the group.

Outside the bowling alley, an assembly of teenage girls were busy trying to find the single best angle from which to take a photo of their group to later uploads to their social media channels and ensure that all of their friends knew that it'd indeed been raining that night, just the off chance they hadn't looked out of a window.

A short distance from the bowling alley was a small, but modern pub, where a number of drunken middle aged men wearing football shirts were jumping up and down while shouting chats at whoever happened to walk past. All the while their wives looked on hoping no one would realise they were with them.

Next to the pub was a popular family restaurant that even at this early hour was already full with the line of those waiting for a table spilling out onto the path outside. While there were a few couples in the queue, many of those waiting were families, the parents of which were looking forward to being able to spend the evening with their children, while also, at the same time, happy that the Christmas holidays were finally over and they'd gone back to school.

At the other side of the complex there stood a building which was much taller than the rest, the town's brand new

friday night

multiplex cinema that'd opened only a few weeks earlier.

This particular night happened to be a busy one for the cinema. It was the opening night of one of the most widely anticipated films for a number of years, and the majority of the buildings twenty-two screens were all showing it.

Anyone who walked through the main entrance doors of the building would've found it difficult to get much further. The main foyer was packed wall to wall with an abundance of people, many of whom had come to watch the new film.

Busy queueing up by the central desk was a group of teenage girls who'd come out straight from school. As slowly, they inched closer towards the desk one of the girls at the back of the group called forward through the crowd. 'Get mine for me. I need to go to the toilet quickly.' Moments later one of her friends called back. 'Alright but be quick, it starts soon.'

The first girl moved away from the rest of her friends and began to make her way towards the small corridor that led off from the main foyer and towards toilets.

As the toilet doors came into view, she passed a man who was stood opposite them waiting for a friend.

Adam Philips was a working professional from the city in his mid-twenties and at nearly six and a half foot, he was of a height that made him stand out from the rest of the crowd.

For as long as he could remember he'd always been taller than anyone else he knew. It was this along with his short brown hair and brown eyes that contributed towards his

three *by* three

considerable success with the opposite sex, particularly when compared with his best friend.

He looked down at his phone as it began to flash in his hand, he'd just received a new message. With a single swipe on the screen, he unlocked the phone and started to read the message;

> Just letting you know, I'm staying with mum tonight,
> I'll see you in the morning xxx

It was from Megan, the woman who had, only recently, become his fiancée after he'd decided to propose to her at a New Years Eve party the week before.

Adam only managed to type the first word of his reply when his friend walked out of the toilets.

'What're you doing?' asked Stuart.

'Oh,' Adam replied as he looked up from his phone. 'Just replying to a message, I'll do it later, it's not important,' and with that, he placed his phone back into his jacket pocket. He knew that Megan knew he was out all night and he'd never been the quickest person at replying to messages anyway. 'Right, let's go,' he continued.

Stuart Wright had been friends with Adam as far back as their first day at primary school when the two first met aged four. Since then they'd both attended the same secondary school, sixth form and University. They'd even studied the

friday night

exact same course and then gone on to work at the same company once they graduated. They'd gotten to know each other so well it was as though they were brothers, and on some days even lovers.

While he was still quite tall, Stuart was slightly shorter than his friend. Unlike Adam he wasn't in a long-term relationship, he'd never quite seemed to have the time to make a real effort with one. His career had always been the most important thing in his life.

Unlike the crowd that surrounded them, Stuart and Adam hadn't just arrived at the cinema. They'd been able to come and watch the film earlier in the day when the cinema was much less busy, and they were now ready to leave.

During the Christmas week while many of their colleagues had been away they'd both agreed to work extra hours, hours which, as they'd found out earlier that day, had been much more profitable than either of them thought. That morning they'd both been summoned to their bosses office where they were given an unexpected five-figure bonus along with the remainder of the day off to celebrate.

As they began to make their way towards the exit, they couldn't help but feel as though it seemed much further away than it did when the'd arrived a few hours earlier. Although earlier there hadn't been an ocean of families young and old they'd needed to wade their way though.

Eventually, they made their way outside after pushing their

three *by* three

way past one final wave of people who were making their way into the comforting warmth of the foyer from the cold outside.

'Pub?' asked Stuart, although he needn't have, he already knew what the answer would be.

'Of course,' replied Adam, predictably so.

They walked forward and made their way towards the edge of the raised platform that the cinema was built upon and looked out at the wide selection of bars and pubs that were within view.

It wasn't long before the weather made them look as though they'd just fallen into a river, the rain was still pounding its way down with such force that it bounced as it hit the ground.

'Actually as you're driving should we just go to that new bar down the road from your house?' Adam asked as he used his jacket sleeve to dry his face.

'That's not a bad idea,' replied Stuart checking the time on his watch. 'It's still quite early. I don't want to spend the night as the designated driver.'

They made their way down the small set of nearby stairs that led down to the main car park. Just why Stuart had decided to park so far away was a mystery to Adam, particularly given that the car park had been empty when they'd arrived, but they were walking for a considerable time before eventually, they reached Stuart's VW Golf.

It was a car that was little over three months old. He'd

friday night

bought it for himself after receiving an inheritance from his parents following their deaths in a plane crash the previous year.

The crash had, ever since it happened, been the subject of many different conspiracy theories. Many of them all came to the same conclusion: that the true events were being covered up by the Government. While the wider public often ignored conspiracy theories, these had found themselves being unexpectedly helped along by the fact that the verdict and conclusions of the official investigation were so full of holes.

Stuart himself was on the fence as to what to believe. He'd attended many of the open sessions during the investigation, heard all of the evidence and read the full conclusion from cover to cover on more than one occasion, but he simply couldn't make up his mind. All he knew was that it was an event which took the lives of both his parents.

As he approached the car, he noticed a problem with one of the front wheels: Its tyre was completely flat.

'Ah look at that,' he said. 'Someone's punctured my tyre.'

'I think that's actually probably your fault,' replied Adam. 'You did drive quite fast down that new road.'

Ignoring his friend Stuart knelt down to get a closer look at the tyre. 'I'm not sure it's going to be safe to drive it like this,' he said as he looked up at Adam with a mix of irritation and (reluctant) guilt showing on his face.

'Don't you have a spare?'

three *by* three

'No. Not in the car anyway, I needed the space. I don't think they'll be a mechanics open at this time either. It's a Friday after all.'

'Well, we'll just have to walk back then.'

'I don't think we've got another option.' He pulled himself up and brushed the dirt of his knees. 'I'll just have to come and sort this out in the morning.'

Although the puncture couldn't help but make him feel frustrated, Stuart was determined not to let something so small dampen his night. And so knowing that by the time they finally had a cold and freshly pulled beer in front of them that they'll have truly earned it, Stuart locked his car and the two of them set off towards the road, on foot but in high spirits.

It took them a little over half an hour to reach the main road that led to the town centre.

The road itself was busy with Friday night traffic and was well lit, as was the left-hand side of it where it was lined with large and expensive set-back houses, every one of which had an immaculately kept front garden separating it from the road.

On the right side of the road however, there was no buildings and no light. Instead, just a deep and dark forest with little more than a single path running through it.

With the rain still incessantly pouring down Adam, who'd been following behind as he didn't know the way, called forward to Stuart. 'How much further is it from here?'

'Well,' replied Stuart as he stopped walking. 'From here

friday night

we've two options.'

'Go on.'

'We can follow this road into town and then back out again. That'll take about an hour.'

'What's the second option?'

'Go through the big, dark and scary forest,' he joked. 'That'll take about half the time. There's probably more cover from the rain that way as well.'

Stuart watched as, without saying anything, Adam set off down the path towards the trees.

'Okay, forest it is then,' he called after him as he began to follow.

'Beer waits for no many my friend.'

It was only a matter of seconds later when Stuart found himself walking straight into the back of Adam as suddenly, and without warning, he stopped.

'What're you doing?' he asked as he watched Adam pull his phone out of his jacket pocket.

'Lighting the way.' Adam tapped on the screen to make the flash at the back of the phone light up.

'Are you scared of the dark now?'

'No,' Adam said as he began walking again. 'I'm just not keen on spending my weekend cleaning dog crap off the bottom of my shoe.'

The torch on the back of Adams phone was only able to light up a few metres of the path in front of them: That was until it wasn't able to light up any of the path in front of them when it ran out of power ten minutes later.

'Okay,' he said. 'I'll admit, now I'm scared.'

'Why? It's only the dark.'

'It's not the dark I'm scared of. It's Megan. She'll think I'm ignoring her.'

'Surely she's used to that by now?'

'Where's that rustling coming from?' asked Adam, changing the subject. He wasn't able to see anything nearby, but he was sure he heard something.

'It's my clothes.'

'Why? What're you doing?'

'I'm trying to find my phone to use as a torch.'

'Oh. Do you mind sending Megan a message for me too?'

'Yeah, sure. As soon as I can find it anyway.'

Adam continued to listen out. He could still hear the rustling of Stuart's clothes, but he was sure he could hear something else, more rustling, coming not from his friend but just off the path, close to where they were stood.

'What's that?'

'What's what?'

'That rustling.'

'It's me. I've just told you.'

'Not that rustling.'

'There isn't any other rustling.'

'Have you found your phone yet?' Adam asked, beginning

to feel his heart rate increase.

'No,' Stuart replied sounding unfazed. 'I think I left it back in the car.'

'Are you going to go back and get it?'

'There's no point now. We're not that far away. I'll just get it when I go back for the car in the morning.'

Adam watched as Stuart began walking again, seemingly unable to hear what he was hearing. Slowly, and reluctantly, he followed behind.

A short while later the rustling returned, this time much closer than it'd been before, close enough so that Stuart was able to hear it too. 'It'll just be the wind. Nothing more,' he called back in a reassuring tone as the area around them fell silent once more.

Further along the path, a single bright light appeared in front of them as if it'd just come out of nowhere.

'It looks as though we're not the only ones taking a shortcut,' muttered Adam under his breath.

'It'll just be someone taking their dog out for a walk or something like that,' replied Stuart. Unlike Adam, he wasn't worried and didn't make any attempt to lower the volume of his voice.

As they continued forwards towards the source of the light, they noticed that it didn't seem to be moving. It was almost as though it was waiting for them to get closer to it.

'Maybe we should turn back?'

three *by* three

'What're you worried about?'

They continued to walk forward until they came within just a few metres of the light.

The first thing they noticed was that it was coming from a single black metal torch. They looked briefly at the gloved hand that was pointing it at them before then looking up at the person who's hand it was.

Stood blocking the path in front of them was a figure dressed entirely in black. All either of them could make out was two bright blue eyes staring at them.

'Hello,' said Stuart, still half expecting there to be a perfectly simple explanation behind what he was looking at.

'I'm not sure you should get any closer,' muttered Adam, having now taken a few step back.

Ignoring him Stuart took another step forward in an attempt to get a better look at the figure, although this time he did so with a clear sense of hesitancy.

'Are... are you... okay?' he asked as he looked back down at the torch. He didn't receive a response, but then he wasn't expecting one either.

Realising Adam may have had a point he took a step backwards.

'Where's it's other hand?' asked Adam as he realised only one was in view.

'I don't know.'

They watched in silence as the figure answered the question

friday night

for them by slowly bringing its other hand around from behind its back.

While it felt much longer to both of them, it only took a fraction of a second for them to notice that in the other hand, the figure was holding an axe.

Almost instinctively they turned and began running in the direction they'd just come from, moving as quickly as they could, and even then trying to run faster still, as the figure gave chase behind them.

'Just get out of this forest,' shouted Stuart at the top of his voice.

'How far ahead are we?' asked Adam in a panic as he attempted to catch his breath without slowing down.

'I don't know. I'm not looking.'

Adam turned his head back. He was only able to get a brief seconds glance, but it was enough for him to know that the figure was moving faster than they were.

'Stuart... It's getting closer.'

'Then get off this path,' he shouted as he changed direction and began to run off into the trees.

Not having heard him clearly Adam continued along the path on his own.

Behind the figure stopped briefly as it decided which of them to follow. A single heartbeat later, it ran into the trees after Stuart.

Ahead Stuart wasn't sure if he was being followed or not,

and if so, how closely. He thought the safest thing for him to do would be to keep running anyway.

At the edge of the forest meanwhile, Adam had now reached the main road. It was only then that he noticed Stuart wasn't with him.

He stopped to catch his breath while he thought about going back to find his friend. It wasn't long however before he realised there was little he'd be able to do, it wasn't a small forest, and he wasn't sure where Stuart had gone off the path. He decided that what he needed to do was go and find help.

He didn't know his way around this part of the town, but he did know that there was a police station in the town centre and that the road he was on would lead him straight to it. As quickly as he could, he made his way across the road, only just avoiding being hit by a number of the cars that beeped at his as they passed, and set off towards help without slowing down.

Further back within the trees Stuart was still running. He was trying to move faster and faster, but it was hard, his shoes didn't have any grip, and in the dark, he couldn't see where any of the muddy patches were to avoid slipping on them.

Eventually though, his luck ran out as he tripped over a fallen branch and then, with a hard thud, he hit the ground just before his vision went blank.

an unexpected reunion

Stuart wasn't sure exactly how long he'd been out for when eventually he regained consciousness.

The first thing he noticed as he opened his eyes was the moon shining brightly above him. It didn't take long for him to realise that he wasn't in the same place he was when he tripped. He wasn't sure how he'd managed to get there, but he was now laid on his back on the forest floor at the edge of a small clearing within the trees.

Unlike the rest of the the forest, the clearing was well lit by the moonlight coming from above, although the denseness of the trees surrounding him made it impossible to see more than just a few metres into the rest of the forest.

By now it'd finally stopped raining and although the dirt in the middle of the opening was still damp and muddy, the

three *by* three

ground that Stuart was laid on had remained dry, having been well protected by the thick leaves of nearby trees.

Although he wasn't sure which part of the forest he was now in or which direction would be the quickest way out of the trees, he felt it was best if he didn't stay around for too much longer.

He attempted to push himself up off the forest floor. Seconds later however, he found himself back on it. He paused for a moment before taking a deep breath and trying again, but it was useless.

He could only presume that he must've injured himself when he tripped because the instant he put any pressure on his right ankle, he felt an immediate deep and sharp pain.

'You're not going to be able to move that easily,' came a sudden but calm voice from within the trees.

Stuart looked around, but he couldn't see anyone nearby.

For a brief second, he hoped it was Adam, but he didn't know if he'd followed him off the path or not, and either way, he knew it couldn't be him. This wasn't a voice he recognised, it wasn't even the voice of a male, it was too soft.

'You've twisted your ankle,' the voice continued. 'If you try to walk now you'll only make it worse.'

He watched as from the other side of the opening a shadow appeared from within the trees. Moments later the shadow was then replaced by the figure that'd been chasing him.

He looked down at the figures hand. It was still holding the

30

an unexpected reunion

axe with a firm grip, only this time the moonlight reflecting off its edge showed just how sharp it was.

The figure took a slow step towards him. Then another. And another.

Taking a deep breath Stuart tried to ignore the pain and push himself up a third time, but again he fell back to the ground.

'Did you not hear me?' The figure took another step closer. 'I just said, you've injured yourself. You won't be able to move that easily.' Another step. And another.

By now the figure was only a single step away from him.

He knew that if he was to be attacked now, then there was nothing he could do. It'd be the end of his life.

Suddenly his mind began flooding with thoughts. The first was of his parents. He wondered if they ever felt like he did now, knowing it was all about to end and there was nothing they could do. Then he thought about everything he'd ever done in his life and finally, everything he hadn't done. He might've had a career that'd gone well, much better than he could ever have hoped for in fact, but there was one thing he didn't have, and that was anyone to miss him.

For the first time in his life he wished that he'd put more effort into finding the one person who was right for him. For the first time in his life, he wished he'd cared more about his personal life.

He took a final deep breath and closed his eyes for what felt like minutes, but couldn't have been more than a few seconds. He waited, expecting to feel the sharp and sudden impact of the axe on his body any moment.

And then nothing.

He felt nothing.

'If I wanted to kill you I already would have.'

He heard a thud as something hard hit the ground beside him.

Slowly he opened his eyes again and looked down at the ground. To his surprise he found himself looking at the axe.

He looked back up at the figure which was still stood staring down at him.

Having seconds earlier been certain it'd be the last thing he ever saw, he could only watch in shock as the figure moved and sat down next to him.

There was little he could do except stare. He tried to think of something to say, anything to say, but he couldn't.

'I recognised you,' said the figure. It spoke with such a soft voice that Stuart couldn't help but think that it sounded friendly.

He was now feeling a level of confusion that only five minutes earlier he'd have thought was impossible for any person to feel. He continued to stare as thoughts about who it could be raced through his mind.

'What...' he finally began. 'What do you mean? You recognised me?'

an unexpected reunion

He watched in silence as the figure bowed its head towards the ground and removed the hood that was covering its head and then the scarf that was covering its face. It then placed them both on the ground before sitting back up and looking Stuart in the face.

He was taken aback to find himself staring at two bright blue eyes, eyes that were staring back into his, eyes that belonged to an average girl of average height.

He was staring at Cleo.

Although he hadn't seen her for some years he still immediately recognised her. They'd both attend the same school and while they'd never been good friends they'd got along and shared classes together.

'I recognised you,' she said again, this time even more softly than before.

Despite the living, breathing evidence in front of him there was still a part of Stuart that couldn't quite believe it was actually her. The way he'd always known her to be just simply didn't fit with what'd just happened. In his mind, she'd always been the quiet and shy girl who kept herself away from any trouble.

'But…' he began without any real idea of what he was going to say. Much to his relief, she interrupted him before he'd a chance to continue.

'I never meant to harm you,' she began. 'I never intended to harm anyone.'

three *by* three

She knew that he'd more than just a few reasons not to believe her and indeed as he looked back at the axe beside him he found it difficult to trust what she was saying. She mightn't have meant any harm at that moment, but she must've earlier on, if she didn't she'd never have chased him, if she didn't she'd never have had the axe to begin with.

'It's not my fault,' she continued.

Stuart remained silent. His head may have been full of questions, but somehow he couldn't work out the words to ask a single one of them.

'What do you mean it isn't your fault?' he asked after a long silence.

'It's the people I live with.'

'Your family?'

'No,' she snapped suddenly. 'I don't have any family. I never have.'

She looked up at him hoping to make eye contact, but he was too busy looking at the axe to notice.

Suddenly the situation occurred to Stuart. Even with himself sat between her and the axe it was no guarantee that he was actually safe. He'd no reason to believe she was telling the truth either.

Without saying anything else he attempted again to push himself up off the ground but, as he fell back down again, he felt even more pain than he'd before. He closed his eyes and took a few deep breaths, trying to ignore the pain.

an unexpected reunion

'Don't keep trying to move. You're only going to make it worse,' she said, attempting to sound comforting.

It didn't work.

Even so, there was little Stuart could do other than watch as she moved to kneel by his ankle. Gently she lifted his right leg and began to rub her fingers around his ankle.

'The good news is that it doesn't feel broken, only sprained.' She reached into one of her pockets and pulled out a large piece of cloth. 'It'll hurt for a few hours, but you should be okay after that... If you rest it anyway.' He continued to watch as she removed his shoe and then his sock to reveal a large circular bruise underneath.

'Who made you?' he asked, trying to take his mind off the pain.

Cleo didn't answer immediately. Instead, she began to create a makeshift bandage from the cloth to wrap around his foot. When she'd tucked the last both of cloth securely under itself, she then pulled his sock and shoe back on as gently as she could.

'They did,' she eventually as she sat back down next to him.

'Who are they?' he pressed, determined to find out exactly what was going on.

'My new family.' She spoke much more quietly now. 'They found me one day.'

It never occurred to Stuart at the time that this wasn't a conversation she'd ever had with anyone before, or that she'd never even had anyone to have this, or indeed any other conversation with.

Even though Cleo knew that there was no one else around she still felt reluctant to talk about them, she knew what'd happen if she was caught doing so.

'What do you mean your new family?' Stuart continued, unaware what was going through her mind.

Cleo took a deep breath. She wasn't sure why but she felt much more comfortable talking to Stuart about it than she'd ever felt even thinking about talking to someone else.

'When we met, when we knew each other, back in school.' She bowed her head towards the ground so that Stuart couldn't see her face. 'I used to live in care, but when I left...'

Although he couldn't see it, he knew she was trying to find back tears, even so, it came as much of a surprise to him as it did to her when he pushed himself closer and put his arm around her shoulder to comfort her.

'When I left I'd nowhere go to, nowhere to live... no one.' She took another deep breath. 'That was when they found me. They gave me a place to live, they gave me food, and they became my family.'

'But who are they?'

'I don't know.'

'You must've some idea of who they are? You live with them.'

'I know some things, but not everything. I overhear things,

see people coming and going, most of it I write down, I've a journal, but they...' She looked up at him. 'They make me do things for them, things I don't want to do, think I shouldn't do.'

'What do you mean? What sort of things?'

'They force me to get money for them... like tonight, that was why I chased after you.' Stuart couldn't help but feel a sudden irresistible urge to check his pockets. 'I haven't taken anything from you, I promise.'

'But why the axe?' he asked, unsure if he actually wanted to know.

'It's a last resort and fear. It's also good for protection: there aren't many people with good intentions around here at night.'

'Have you...'

'No,' she interrupted. 'I've never used it to kill anyone anyway.'

Stuart wasn't sure he wanted to know exactly what she meant.

'What do these people actually want anyway?'

'I don't know everything. I'm kept out of most of it,' she began. 'It started as petty crime, things like this but then, from what I've overheard, it's become more. I think they're involved in plots, terrorist plots.' She bowed her head towards the ground again, this time in shame that she'd ever been involved with such people. 'I don't know everything, I've written things down, notes, what I overhear, but I haven't worked it out yet, not all of it.'

three *by* three

'Why can't you just leave them?' He knew the second he asked that it was a stupid question and as he found out moments later, it wasn't a question she needed to answer with words.

He watched as she sat back up and pulled up her sleeve to reveal an arm covered in burns, bruises and deep cuts.

Reaching out Stuart held her arm up in front of himself to get a closer look at the extent of her injuries. It was evident from the gasp she let out as he touched her skin that she was in pain, but she made no attempt to move her arm.

'They're all from them,' she said. 'They'd kill me if I were to leave. I know too much, much of which they don't even know I know.' Gently she moved her arm and pulled her sleeve back down.

They sat in silence, both of them in deep thought and hoping the other would break the silence, this time however, neither of them did.

As would be expected on a Friday night, the reception room of the local police station was full of drunks who'd been arrested for everything from exposing themselves in public to being sick over a waiter after trying, unsuccessfully, to mix just a few too many different drinks.

By the door that led towards the cells, there were two men shouting inaudible insults both each other and the officers that were escorting them. Sat on a chair a short distance from them

an unexpected reunion

was another man whose face was dripping with blood from a cut on his forehead, although he seemed to be too busy babbling exactly what he thought of someone under his breath to notice the bleeding.

In the centre of the room was a large reception desk, behind which a single officer was sat frantically working through the paperwork to process that night's arrests. She hardly flinched when a few seconds later, the entrance doors opposite her desk smashed open as Adam ran in.

'The forest…' he panted as he approached the desk.

'Can I help you?' asked the officer as she sat back in her chair and looked up at him. She couldn't help but presume he must've been drinking as he stood there panting and trying to catch his breath.

'The forest…'

'The forest?' she questioned, hoping that his answer would at least be amusing. 'I think perhaps you've had a bit too much to drink sir. Maybe you should sit down and rest for a while,' she continued as she made her way around the desk.

'Attack.' Adam caught his breath and continued. 'Armed attack… in the forest.'

Almost instantly the officer's expression changed from one of mild amusement to one of fear and worry: This wasn't the first time that someone had said that.

'Which forest is this?' she asked with a sense of urgency.

'The one that runs along the main road.'

three *by* three

'How many attackers?'

'I only saw one. I managed to run but the attacker... it followed my friend into the trees. They were armed with an axe.'

'Excuse me one moment please.' With that she disappeared through the door that was behind her desk.

The room the door led to was the police stations central control room. It was a room full of closely packed desks, all of which were topped with mountains of paperwork that reached into the air, making it difficult to see clearly across the room.

Despite it being a Friday evening every desk was taken. While some them were being used by officers who usually worked the late shift, most were being utilised by those catching up with work on minor crimes that'd taken place over the Christmas period when they were short staffed.

As the officer from reception walked in the room was full of talking, some of it coming from those busy talking on the phone and some from the group bunched up around a water cooler taking a quick break to talk about the cases they were working on. One by one however, the room fell slowly silent as her colleagues noticed her standing there with a concerned look.

'There's been another attack... just now, the same forest.'

At the back of the room, a tall senior man who'd been busy working at his desk stood up. This man was the police station's, superintendent. 'We need to get there now,' he said in

an unexpected reunion

a commanding voice. 'Everyone is to come. We must find that attacker this time,' he added as he made his way over to the officer from reception. 'Make sure the armed unit are ready as soon as possible,' he instructed her. 'They're to meet us there.'

'I used to think you were cute.' Back in the forest, Cleo had finally broken the silence. 'Back when we were both at school,' she continued, unsure exactly how he'd respond.

They were still sat together at the edge of the forest cleaning, although neither had been able to look the other in the face. Instead, they'd both been staring at the other side of the clearing in deep thought.

Stuart didn't respond to her straight away, but he did look at her with a slight and subtle smile, although Cleo was too busy looking in the other direction to notice.

'It's been a long time since we last met.'

'Six years,' she said. 'I dropped out of school when I was 17.'

'You just left one day.' He began as though he wanted to ask her what happened. 'No one ever knew where you went.' Suddenly realised he already knew the answer. 'I'm sorry, I shouldn't...'

'It's fine,' she interrupted. 'It's me that should be sorry.' She took a deep breath before changing the subject. 'How did your life work out?' she asked with genuine interest.

'It's good. I've a good job, I earn a lot, I get to enjoy life, live it the way I want to,' he hesitated as he thought about the one thing he didn't have. 'Well almost anyway.'

'Do you not have a wife?' she asked.

'No.'

'Husband?'

'No.'

'Fiancee? Girlfriend?'

'I've never found anyone who was right. Not that I've ever really spent time looking.'

'Do you spend a lot of time with your family?'

'No.' He paused. 'I don't have any left. I was an only child, as were my parents, and they...' He paused again. 'They both died in a plane crash last year.'

'I'm sorry,' said Cleo.

Stuart lifted his leg to take the pressure off of his injured ankle. Cleo looked over and stared at it.

'If it isn't much better in the morning you should probably see a doctor about it,' she said sounding apologetic. 'I don't think it's broken, but I'm not an expert.'

He looked at it again himself and laughed. 'I'd probably have to tell them how it happened,' he said.

'I suspect... that'd mean I'll be handed in then?'

They looked up into each other's eyes. As they did, Stuart noticed a single tear running down her face. He wasn't sure why but he went with his impulse and used his finger to clear it up. 'Is that not better than going back to them though? You can bring an end to this, turn them all in.'

an unexpected reunion

'Anything would be better.' She paused. 'All I want is to live a normal life and have freedom to do what I want: like you do.' Another tear began to run slowly down her face. 'But this is much bigger than that, there is more to it than that, I don't know exactly what it is, but it'd take more than just me to end it.'

Stuart looked back down at his injured ankle, still bound up in cloth, and then back up at Cleo. In the distance, they could hear rustling from within the trees.

'That'll probably be someone looking for you,' she said looking into the trees. 'That person who was with you, he must've got help.'

'You could always run.'

'I can't from them. I never can.'

'But you can from here.'

She looked down at his ankle and then at him, all the while the rusting was getting closer and closer to the opening. As much as she didn't want to get caught, she felt reluctant to leave him injured.

'But what about you?' she asked. 'I can't just leave you here, not like this.'

'If anyone asks I'll say I tripped and never saw you.'

Cleo knew she didn't have long to make a decision.

Somewhat hesitantly she stood up and took a few steps forward before turning back and looking down at Stuart.

'Thank you,' she said. 'I'm sorry about your ankle.'

three *by* three

A light appeared from within the trees, followed by a voice. 'This is the police. Please make your presence known, we've medical help for you if you need it.'

'It sounds as though they're looking for you,'

'Then you need to go quickly.'

She turned and began to walk towards the trees when suddenly;

'Cleo', Stuart called after her.

'Yes?' she said turning back again.

'It was good to see you again.'

At that moment the light shone into the opening. Without saying another word Cleo turned and ran into the trees away from the opening and the light.

Stuart remained silent and still as a police officer carrying a torch walked into the opening. Although he shone the light around, he never noticed Stuart lying on the floor, and after a few seconds, he continued walking back into the darkness at the other side. Before long another three officers also walked into the opening and then back into the trees, following the first officer. As they passed, Stuart looked up and noticed that all three of them were carrying guns by their side.

He stifled his breathing in the hope none of them would look back. If they did, they'd surely notice him instantly. He wasn't worried about what'd happen if they did, after all, they were there to help him, but he thought it'd be best for Cleo if he didn't have to answer any question about what'd happened,

an unexpected reunion

particularly given that she'd left the axe behind.

He waited for a moment after they'd passed him before making another attempt to stand up. Although his ankle was still hurting him significantly, Cleo's makeshift bandage was enough to give him the support he needed to pull himself up. Once he'd got his balance, he began, slowly, to walk into the trees.

A few moments later he started as from the other side of the forest he heard the distinct sound of two gunshots followed immediately by a high pitched scream.

Immediately he turned and began running in the direction that the scream had come from, ignoring the agony that was throbbing in his ankle.

At the source of the gunshots were the four police officers that'd walked past Stuart in the opening. One of them was holding out in front of them the gun that the shots had come from.

'Follow the sound of that scream,' he said to the other officers as he began walking in the direction he was pointing his gun.

At the same time further ahead Cleo was running as fast as she could, unsure where she could go or what she could do.

'Are we shooting to kill?', asked one of the officers.

'Only if we're attacked first,' replied the first officer. 'We've permission to shoot to injure though. These attacks must be stopped.'

three *by* three

Cleo stopped running to catch her breath, all the time looking around frantically to see if anyone else was close by. She could hear the trees and bushes rustling in all directions. Cautiously she took a few steps back and leant against a nearby tree.

Above her, there was a small opening in the canopy that let in just enough moonlight for her to be able to see what'd happened to her arm. One of the bullets had hit her.

As she looked down, she saw blood dripping onto the ground from the large wound just below her shoulder. She put her other hand over the wound but instantly removed it as an impulse reaction to the sting.

Trying to control her breathing and catch her breath she let her hands rest by her side before letting out another sharp scream as she felt one of them being grabbed.

She turned around and found herself face to face with Stuart once more.

'I used to think you were quite cute too.'

They smiled briefly at each other before noticing the light from the officer's torch approaching them. Without any more conversation, they started running away from the light together.

Despite their injuries, they managed to create some distance between themselves and the officers, and then, without warning, Cleo disappeared from sight.

Stuart stopped and looked beside him. There was a large

an unexpected reunion

ditch several metres deep and at the bottom, Cleo.

He looked behind him. He wasn't sure how far ahead they were, but he knew he'd to move quickly. He climbed to the bottom of the ditch to find Cleo lying in pain.

'Get yourself out,' she said feeling dazed.

'I'm not leaving you here.'

Suddenly the ditch filled with light. He looked up and found all four of the officers staring down at them.

With no other option, he picked Cleo up in his arms and made his way across to the other, less steep, side of the ditch. Being careful not to drop her he climbed his way back up before breaking into a run.

'There's two of them,' said one of the officers. 'There are two attackers.' All four of them set off in pursuit.

Ahead Stuart wasn't sure where he was, but he kept running anyway, hoping to find the edge of the forest. And then, before long he saw lights and ran towards them.

He didn't know which part of the main road they'd come out on, but they'd made it out of the trees.

A short time later the four officers also made it to the main road but as they looked around neither Stuart or Cleo were in sight.

chapter four
the **top** office

Moments after it had been delivered by the local paper boy, Sir Spencer Stout walked into his large open plan kitchen with that morning's broadsheet folded up under his arm.

It was now Saturday morning, and while for many it meant a chance for a well-deserved lie in and rest after a long week at work, for Spencer it meant another early morning and another full day in the office.

Spencer lived in a large detached and ageing house just outside the small town of Weybridge in Surrey on one of the capitals more exclusive (and expensive) commuter routes.

Although his house had a total of six bedrooms, only one of them was ever used. He lived alone and had done so for over two decades, although there was once a time in his life when it looked as though it could've gone a very different way.

the top office

He'd fallen in love with a woman called Elizabeth who he'd been set to marry. Only a few weeks before their wedding however, his job got in the way, and they both felt it'd be best if they went their separate ways.

In his heart he knew he still loved her and always had. He'd always known it wouldn't take much time or effort to find out where she was and see her again, but he knew doing so would put her life in danger.

Spencer kept a constant reminder of the life he could've had on top of a small table just a few feet from his front door. Held within a small and well polished golden frame was a photo of the two of them together. It was always the last thing he saw when he left his house and the first thing he saw when he returned again, although never had he stopped wishing he was coming home to the actual person rather than just an old photo.

He made himself a cup of tea and sat down at the dining table in the middle of the room just as the antique grandfather clock chimed to announce that it was now seven o'clock. He unfolded the newspaper and opened it up on the table in front of him. Almost immediately his eyes were drawn to the morning's headline;

PRIME MINISTER CONFIRMS TERROR SUSPICIONS

It was printed in solid bold lettering just above a picture of what appeared to be burning wreckage of some sort.

three *by* three

Spencer didn't need to read the accompanying article or even look at the picture to know exactly what the headline was referring to. Nevertheless, he began to read the article anyway, hoping greatly that what he was about to read wasn't going to mean months of late nights at work.

The Prime Minister last night confirmed the circumstances around the tragedy of flight BV28 are to be reevaluated to examine the possibility of terrorist actions being responsible for the downing of the plane last March.

The original accident report into the crash of the flight from London to New York, published last month concluded that the flight was brought down by a leak within one of the engines fuel systems, although this has been disputed by a number of aviation experts.

In his announcement made last night at a press conference attended by some of the family and friends of those onboard the flight, the Prime Minister confirmed that he has in the past week been made aware of new evidence relating to the flight and that a new full-scale review of this along with all previous evidence will be carried out by the Independent Security Service (ISS) with a full report due to be published before next year's General Election.

It was the last paragraph in particular that Spencer was hoping he wouldn't see printed.

He'd met with the Prime Minister over lunch only a few

days earlier to discuss the matter, in fact he was the one aware of the new evidence in the first place. Spencer had however also urged the Prime Minister not to make any public announcement about a new investigation and, in particular, who'd be carrying it out.

The circumstances that surround the crash had, ever since the day the tragedy took place, attracted large amounts of media speculation and public attention, speculation and attention that often got in the way of the investigations being carried out.

There was a part of Spencer that couldn't help but think this latest announcement was just the Prime Ministers way of showing that the enormous amounts of public money spent on setting up a new security service had been worthwhile, particularly with an election only a year away.

With a short sigh, Spencer folded the paper back up, poured the remainder of his tea down the sink and went to walk out of the house, picking up his coat and bag from the hallway oh his way. Before closing the door, he took a last look back at the photograph on the table and smiled at it.

Spencer was the director of the Independent Security Service, a new organisation that'd been set up only two years earlier as a less political alternative to the already established MI5 and MI6.

Although they still took some direction from the central Government, the ISS were free to investigate whatever, and whoever, they chose. It was something that was starting to annoy certain political figures who'd been the subject of investigations into corruption and, more recently, a possible cover-up of the true events of flight BV28.

While his job did mean he often had to work on weekends, it was also a job that came with a considerable number of benefits. His favourite perk was that he'd his own personal parking space in central London. It meant he was always able to drive to work rather than be forced to rely on the less than perfect trains into the capital each morning.

That particular morning was a quiet one on the roads, and so it wasn't long before he was pulling into his space within a secure underground car park. Unfortunately, while the traffic may have been favourable, it still took him another half hour before making it up the maze of lifts and through the security checkpoint before finally arriving at the ISS lobby on the 45th floor.

The tallest building in the east of London was, by some distance, the Canary Wharf tower within the Canary Wharf business complex. It was a building which boasted some of the best views in the city, but for the past couple of years the top six floors had been heavily guarded and shut off to the public. They were the place the ISS called home and a place where each and every phone conversation could be listened to, email read and signal traced to an accuracy measured in millimetres.

The choice of location was mainly down to the need to

the top office

have somewhere high up to keep a large, diverse and expensive (but useful) collection of ariels, radars and equipment.

There was another, even taller, building in the West that'd also been considered and while the owners of that building were initially keen on the idea, they soon lost their cooperative stance following a games night with top Government officials during which one of them became convinced the Foreign Secretary had cheated during a game of Monopoly.

Spencer's office was at the top of the building and thanks to its floor to ceiling glass windows it was an office that came with vast panoramic views of the capital, or as he preferred to call it, his thinking space.

After saying good morning to those he passed in the lobby, he entered another lift that would take him to his office. As the lift reached the top floor, he walked out into a small reception room. 'Good morning,' he said to his secretary as he passed by her desk.

'Good morning sir,' she replied. 'Mr Jones is waiting in your office for you sir.'

'Already? It's still early.'

'Yes sir. He said it was urgent.'

'Alright, thank you.'

At that moment another lift arrived, and a woman in her late twenties walked out.

'Good morning,' said the woman.

three *by* three

'Ah Marley, good morning,' he smiled at her.

Despite her young age Marley Fayette was one of the ISS's most senior agents (a job she'd got in no small part due to her superior intellect) and someone who reported directly to Spencer.

'I hear your colleague is already waiting for us,' continued Spencer as he led the way down a nearby corridor to his office.

'He's been here all night,'

'Really? What was he doing?'

'Following that girl.'

'He still thinks it's her?'

'He thinks he's found someone she's working with.'

'Well let's find out.'

They'd reached the door to his office. As they walked in a tall man also in his late twenties who'd been sat waiting for them stood up with an envelope in his hand. Much like Marley, Zachary Jones was also one of the ISS's most senior people.

'Good morning sir,' said the man.

'Zachary,' Spencer nodded at him. 'About this girl, you can't still be serious can you?'

'Sir?' He sat back down as Spencer and Marley also took a seat.

'She's a young girl.'

'I think I've found evidence though sir.'

'Is that what that's?' asked Spencer pointing at the

envelope.

'No sir. I'm still writing a report on the evidence. These are stills taken from CCTV cameras last night though, they show her with another person.'

Spencer reached out and took the envelope from Zachary. After emptying the contents onto the desk in front of him, he held up one of the photos. It was a photo of Clec.

'This is who you think brought a plane down on her own?' he asked sounding doubtful.

Zachary reached forward and picked up another photo, this one of Cleo being carried by Stuart across the cinema car park the night before.

'She was with someone else last night.'

Spencer looked at the photo and then up at Zachary. 'Do you know who the other person is?'

Marley interjected. 'We don't even know who the girl is yet.'

'It's hard to trace someone who doesn't seem to officially exist,' replied Zachary.

'What do you mean?' asked Spencer.

'I've been trying to follow her, but she doesn't seem to live anywhere. There's nothing I can use to trace her.'

'Do you know where they both are now?'

'Yes sir. I followed them back to a car park last night, and I checked this morning, they're still there, they slept in the back of a car.'

'Do you know who the car belongs to?'

three _by_ three

'I presume it's his.'

'Can you not find out who he is through the numberplate?' suggested Marley.

'That's a good point,' said Spencer. 'Well... Zachary?'

'Yes sir.'

'Marley have you got any further with our other line of enquiry?'

'There's evidence to suggest that the Ministry of Defence knew there was a plot.'

'Do you know if they took any action to prevent it?'

'It would've been dealt with by MI5, but they've been reluctant to share any information with us.'

'What about other Government departments?'

'They're not really that keen on us investigating them.'

'Okay. I'll talk to the Prime Minister later on and see if I can get the information you need released.'

'Thank you.'

'Zachary,' he said turning his attention back to him.

'Yes sir?'

'Are you certain this girl is a valid line of inquiry?'

'Yes I am sir.'

'Well it seems unlikely that she could do it on her own, but if there's a chance she's working with other people then you may have a point. Trace the numberplate and bring them both in.'

'But sir,' he replied.

the **top** office

'Yes?'

'Shouldn't we find more evidence before we do that?'

'You've just said yourself that you think she's the one and that you've evidence.'

'But not enough yet sir.'

'You seem reluctant to move this forward... there isn't more to this is there?'

'No sir. I just think...' He stopped talking as Spencer raised his hand.

'Find them,' he said. 'I'm sure it can only be easier for you to find evidence once they've been questioned.'

'Yes sir.'

'Good.' He stood up and walked over to the door to hold it open for them. 'Well you've both got things to be working on today.'

'Thank you,' said Marley as she left.

'Zachary?' said Spencer noticing he hadn't moved from his chair.

'Oh... yes sir,' he replied standing up.

'Is that a personal phone?' asked Spencer suspiciously as he saw him pocketing his phone.

'Yes sir... I'm sorry sir... It's my mother. She's in hospital.'

'No personal phones at work. No exceptions.'

'Yes sir... I understand.'

As Zachary left the room Spencer returned to sit at his desk. He looked up at the calendar on the wall and sighed as he noticed the date. He sat contemplating the thoughts on his mind for a short while as he looked out at his view of the city before accepting there was something much more important that he needed to do that day.

Leaving his office, he made his way back to his secretaries desk. 'What do I have scheduled for this afternoon?' he asked her.

'You're meant to be meeting with the Prime Minister at 2 pm sir.'

'Reschedule it for tomorrow and leave today blank. There's somewhere else I need to be later on.'

'Yes sir, I understand. I'll sort that for you.'

'Thank you.'

At the end of a corridor on the floor below Marley was sat working in her office. There was a knock on the door and Spencer walked in before taking a seat next to her.

'You don't have to be here today if you don't want to be,' he said, speaking in a much softer and sympathetic tone than he in his office.

'I know,' she replied. 'But it's what he'd have wanted.'

'That's true. Your father did always have a good work ethic.' He paused. 'But he never made the mistake I did.'

'What was that?'

'He never put work before his family and friends.'

'I miss him this year... I mean I've missed him every year but this more than before.'

the top office

'Are you planning to go and lay flowers later?'

She looked him in the face. 'I want to but it… it doesn't feel right this year, not without my mother there as well.'

'She'd have wanted you to lay them for both of you.'

'I know. She always asked me if I would when she was gone, and I always said yes but it's twenty years this time.'

'That's all the more reason to.'

She nodded gently at him and smiled before turning her focus back to her computer screen.

'What're you working on?' he asked with interest in an attempt to change the subject.

'I'm trying to access emails sent between senior civil servants at the Ministry of Defence.'

'Another brick wall?'

She nodded. 'They use the same encryption we do.'

'So much for all the talk about sharing information for the greater good. Sometimes I feel as though there are some in the Government who actually want us to be ineffective.'

'There was something I wanted to talk to you about… in private.'

'Certainly.'

'It's Zachary,' she began. 'I still can't shake off the feeling that there is something else going on with him.'

'As I said to you last time, he's been throughout the same vetting process as you, me and everyone else who works here,' said Spencer. 'Having said that though, other people have said things since you first did and it does seem strange that he thinks a young girl could bring down a plane on her own,' he paused and thought. 'And then he seemed reluctant to find her.'

'Should I look into it?'

'No,' he said. 'Not you. Your skills would be wasted on it. I'll find someone else to look into Zachary, but it might be best if you were to look into this girl too. If you've the time of course?'

'I can do that.'

'It needs to stay between us though. If something is going on with him it's best if he doesn't know we're looking into it.'

'I understand.'

'Good,' he said as he stood back up. 'Well, I must get back to work.'

'Sir,' she called after him.

'Yes?'

'Spencer,' she continued as she stood up. 'I don't want to go there alone.'

'Okay,' he said as he walked towards her. 'Come with me later when I go. I've my own respects to pay after he saved my life.'

'You're my boss though.'

'Yes, I am… but you're also my friend.'

chapter five
saturday morning

It was much warmer and drier than the previous night suggested it might've been and the sun shone brightly over Parkview Drive reflecting off the metallic paint of the cars parked in the driveways, many of which were in the fifty thousand plus section of the market. This wasn't a street whose residents faced a struggle to get by on the bare minimum.

Number 31 was a large recently built detached house about half way down the street. It had a basic, but well kept, front garden and much like the neighbours, it's grass that was bright green and neatly cut.

Already parked on the double flagstone driveway was a brand new (and highly optioned) estate that had cost its owner close to a hundred thousand and it wasn't long before this car was joined by another of similar style and cost.

Out of the second car came a tall and casually dressed woman in her mid-twenties. It was Adam's fiancée Megan, and as she walked towards the front door, she wore a worried look.

The interior of the house fitted with its exterior. Again it was basic but well kept and clean.

'It's me,' Megan called out as she hung her jacket up on a block of hooks next to the door. 'I came as soon as I got your text.' She flicked off her shoes and continued through a nearby door into the lounge.

Adam was already sat in the room, but he was too busy staring intently at the news on the TV in front of him to acknowledge her presence.

'Are you okay?' she asked, sitting down next to him.

He didn't respond.

Wondering what he could be so focused on that he'd completely ignore her, Megan turned to look at the TV herself. She froze almost immediately as she read the headline that was crawling its way along the bottom of the screen;

HOMICIDE INVESTIGATION OPENED
FOLLOWING NIGHT TIME ATTACK

Megan did, and said, nothing as she continued to watch.

'It's in this forest behind me,' began the on-screen reporter. They were stood at the edge of a forest, the same forest that Adam and Stuart had been in the night before and behind

saturday morning

them were a number of police officers busy taping off the area. 'That last night a series of events took place that have this morning prompted local police to launch an investigation into a possible homicide. At this current early stage, little information has been released by police, but they believe that there are two attackers, both of which are yet to be caught. The public has been asked to remained vigilant at this time, both of the attackers are presumed to be armed and dangerous and shouldn't be approached under any circumstances.'

Megan looked briefly across at Adam who was still staring at the screen in disbelief. Rather than attempt a conversation, she decided to put her arm around him in comfort before moving her attention back to the TV.

'At this stage,' the reporter continued. 'Police are in the process of searching for an individual who's believed to have been the target of last night's events.' An old photo of Stuart appeared on the screen next to the reporter. 'If you've seen this man or have any information regarding these attacks then the police are requesting that you contact them directly as soon as you can do so.'

At the other side of town, the leisure park was an entirely different place to what it'd been the night before. The warm rays of the Saturday morning sun had meant most of the puddles left by the previous night's downpour had now disappeared and, except for a single VW Golf parked on its own, the car park was now also completely empty.

Stood next to this car was a short and chubby looking parking inspector who was busy watching while taller and thinner colleague finish fitting a clamp to one of the wheels.

'Is this not a bit unfair?' he asked as the other inspector stood back up. 'I mean, the driver is sat in the car.' He pointed at Stuart who was sat asleep in the driver's seat with his head resting up against the window. 'And he does have a flat tyre too.'

'It doesn't matter whether it's fair or not. He overstayed the time that he paid for,' said the other inspector as he tapped on the windscreen where Stuart had stuck (a now expired) parking ticket. 'Rules are rules, and it's our job to enforce them. He's got a clamp, and now he's getting a fine as well.'

Looking pleased with himself he stuck a penalty notice onto the windscreen before walking away towards a small office at the other side of the car park, his colleague following behind.

It was a short while later when Stuart woke up. After taking a look around to ensure that nobody else was nearby, he finished off the bottle of water in the cup holder next to him and got out of the car to open the back door at the other side.

Cleo was laid across the back seats with her head by the open door. Most of her was covered up under an old blanket so that anyone walking past wouldn't notice she was there.

She opened her eyes and then shut them again almost

saturday **morning**

immediately to block out the sun above. After a few seconds, she slowly opened them again as Stuart moved to block out the light.

'Where am I?' she asked with only vague memories of the previous night.

'My car,' Stuart replied. 'We're a couple of miles away from the forest.'

'I don't,' she began. 'I don't remember what happened, not most of it. I remember you, and then I remember falling. There were bright lights. I heard a gunshot.' She sat up as Stuart climbed into the back of the car next to her. 'Did you... did you carry me all of the way here?'

'Yes.' His answer was short. 'I didn't have a choice. You fell and injured yourself. I couldn't just leave you there.'

By now the adrenaline from the night before had worn off, and Stuart was starting to feel the pain in his ankle. However much pain he felt however, it was nothing compared to the pain Cleo was feeling from the open wound on her arm.

The morning light meant that for the first time they were able to see exactly what'd happened. As they looked down at her arm, they noticed a large an uneven hole in her shirt, the edge of which were stained a dark red from her blood. Luckily for Cleo the bullet had only left a flesh wound and while there was a deep cut she knew that it'd eventually heal.

Stuart reached into the front of the car to retrieve a small first aid box from the glove compartment. He took out a small antiseptic wipe and removed it from its wrapper before using it to clean the wound on her arm. Although the alcohol on the wipe stung as it touched her, she didn't make any attempt to stop him or move her arm.

'Why did you come back for me?'

'Because,' he began. 'I don't know… It just felt like the right thing to do.'

'But there were armed police searching for me?'

'I know.'

She smiled at him, but he didn't notice.

'I think I was hit,' she said as she looked back down at the arm.

'At least it was only the side of your arm. It would have been much worse if it'd gone through it.'

'Thank you,' she said after a short pause.

'What for?'

'Coming back.'

Stuart didn't reply. Instead, he finished cleaning the wound before taking a large patch from the first aid box and using it to cover the cut.

'So… what do we do now?' she continued.

'I'm not sure.'

'Is it…' she began, unable to think how best to word what she wanted to ask. 'Would it be possible…'

'Possible?' he questioned.

'To stay…'

saturday **morning**

'Yes.'

'Yes, what?'

'Stay with me,' said Stuart softly. 'At least for now anyway.'

'Thank…' she began, but before she'd a chance to finish he interrupted her;

'You need a change in your life.' He took a deep breath. 'And perhaps so do I.'

'What is it that you do?' Cleo asked sounding genuinely interested.

'I work for a bank in the city.'

'That doesn't sound that bad.'

'It pays well, but it's not always the most interesting life.'

By now it was mid-morning, and other cars were starting to appear. Close to where they were a family of four climbed out of their estate and walked past them as they made their way towards the cinema.

'We should probably get away from here,' Cleo said. 'It's going to start getting busy soon.'

'That's not going to be that easy. I've got a flat tyre,' he said as he climbed back out of the car and noticed for the first time that he'd also now been clamped too. 'And now I've got a clamp as well.'

'Don't you have a spare wheel?'

'No… I needed to boot space.'

'Well where's the nearest garage then?'

'It's about half a mile away.'

three *by* three

'Let's go there then,' she said cheerfully as she climbed out of the car. 'We can't waste too much time. The police are probably still looking for me.'

Stuart looked down at the ground and noticed a phone lying face down next to his wheel. As he bent town to pick it up, he realised it was his phone, the same one that'd fallen out of his pocket the night before.

Although the screen was smashed the phone itself worked perfectly and, as he pushed the home button the screen lit up with a message telling him he'd 28 missed calls, all of them from Adam. Not being sure how best to explain what'd happened, he decided to leave it until later. He put the phone into his pocket and then walked around to the boot of his car to take out a spare jacket which he handed to Cleo.

'You should probably put this on,' he said. 'That arm is going to raise more than just a few questions if anyone sees it.'

Nodding in agreement, she put the jacket on. 'Are you okay to be walking on your ankle?' she asked. 'It didn't look very good last night. You should probably be resting it as much as you can.'

'It's a bit stiff, but I'll have to manage, I don't have another choice,' he replied. 'Are you okay to walk yourself?'

'I'll manage.'

Although it was close by it still took them nearly an hour to walk to the garage. Both had needed to stop multiple times to take the weight off their injuries.

saturday morning

The garage was made up of two buildings. The first was a large brick structure that had a number of metal shutter doors on the front that faced the nearby road, all of which were open with mechanics busy working on cars in every bay. The second building was the garages reception and was an almost conservatory like extension that came off the side of bigger building.

Stuart and Cleo stopped behind a small fence at one side of the garage forecourt, out of sight from those in the building.

'Do you have any money with you?' Cleo asked.

'Not cash. I have my credit card though.'

'It'd probably be better if you went and sorted this out on your own.'

Stuart agreed and set off towards the building with a limp. As he approached the first set of shutters, a short man in his mid-forties wearing deeply oil stained overalls walked out of the reception building.

'Excuse me,' Stuart called. 'Do you work here?'

'Yes mate,' the man replied. 'I own this garage. What can I do for you?'

'I've got a flat tyre. I think I'm going to need a new one.'

'Right okay. Do you have the car with you?' the man asked as he attempted to avert his gaze away from the bloodstained patches on Stuarts jacket.

'It's in the car park at the cinema. I wasn't able to drive it how it is.' Stuart looked down to see what the man had been

69

staring at. His jacket looked as though it'd been worn during a car crash. 'I tried to take the wheel off myself, but I cut myself. Didn't have the right tools,' he added, trying to think quickly.

'Well,' said the man sounding unconvinced. 'I'm sure that one of the boys could come and give you some help. Wouldn't be for an hour or so though.'

'Yeah, that'd be fine.'

'Do you know the sort of tyre you need?'

'Just a basic one, it's for the new Golf.'

'I'm sure we've got a few of those in stock. Come into the office for a minute and I'll sort it out for you.'

At the other side of the forecourt, Cleo watched as Stuart and the garage's owner walked into the office. It was only ten minutes before Stuart reappeared and walked over to her with a confused look on his face.

'Is everything sorted then?' she asked sounding hopeful.

'Not quite.'

'Why? What's happened?'

'My card's been blocked,' he said holding up his platinum American Express. 'I've no idea why.'

Cleo moved her gaze to the left of Stuart and noticed a pile of old scrap wheels close to where they were both stood. 'I think I can sort this out,' she said with a smile on her face.

Inside the garage the mechanics were busy concentrating, if they weren't they might've noticed the stray wheel roll past them *before* it hit a large collection of tools and objects at the

saturday **morning**

other side of the garage with a loud and sudden crash that was followed immediately by a groan and a grunt as a number of those objects then fell on top of someone who was waiting to pick their car up.

Almost at once everybody stopped what they were doing and went to see what'd happened.

With a short window of opportunity, Cleo ran into the garage and picked up a new wheel along with a spare tool kit that was lying around and, with one last grab, the remainder of somebody's lunch from a side workbench. Stuart watched from the fence in disbelief. Somehow not a single person had seen her.

'I told you I could sort it,' she said with a slight, but justified, smugness in her tone as she handed him the wheel and tool kit to carry. 'Roast chicken,' she continued as she took a bite from the lunch. 'It's not bad.'

Being weighed down by the wheel and the tools it took them even longer to make their way back to the car park and by the time they eventually did, it was considerably busier.

'Have you got everything you need?' asked Cleo through a mouthful of apple as she finished off the rest of the stolen lunch.

'Yeah. I think so.' Wasting no time Stuart got straight to his knees by the wheel. 'Nice job getting the tools.'

'Thanks,' she replied. 'I wouldn't have thought you'd approve of that method.'

three *by* three

'Usually I don't think I would have,' he looked up at her and smiled. 'But I don't think there was any other way.'

Over at the other side of the car park the two inspectors who'd earlier clamped Stuart were returning to their office at the end of their lunch break. While the taller of the two had already finished his food, the shorter was still clutching a bag of fresh doughnuts in his hand.

They sat down at their desks and began looking over the CCTV screens that were in front of them. It wasn't long before the larger of the two noticed what Stuart was doing.

'Hey look at this,' he said to his colleague while attempting to swallow a particularly chewy piece of doughnut.

'He's taking that bloody clamp off,' said the other as he leant in to look at the screen.'

'What do we do?'

'We need to stop him.'

'Can I finish this doughnut first?'

'No.'

'But it's got extra caramel in it.'

'Finish it off later. Come on.'

The taller of the inspectors set off running out of the office and, after a few seconds his colleague followed, although much more slowly and with a half eaten doughnut in his hand.

Stuart was just finishing fitting the last of the screws on the new wheel when Cleo looked over and noticed the two inspectors walking towards them: One taking small bites of his doughnut with each step he took.

'Stuart…' she said firmly.

'Yeah?' he replied, his focus still on the wheel.

'Stuart!' she said again, this time much louder.

'What is it?' He looked up at her and watched as she pointed at the two men approaching them. 'Shit,' he said as he realised what was happening. 'Get into the car,' he instructed her with a sense of urgency in his voice.

'What about those two?' she replied.

'I think I can sort this out,' he replied gleefully with a smile on his face.

Cleo watched as Stuart threw the tools away from the car before picking up the wheel he'd just removed off and rolling it towards the inspectors.

'Oi! You two!' shouted the taller of the two as he tripped over the wheel, bringing his colleague down with him.

'My doughnut!' cried the (now distraught) shorter inspector.

'Stop them you idiot… never mind your doughnut.'

'But it had extra caram…'

'… JUST STOP THEM!'

Stuart climbed into the driver's seat and started the engine. 'Well it worked for you,' he said to Cleo as they drove off.

After pulling themselves up off the ground, the inspectors could only watch as Stuart and Cleo drove off towards the main road.

three *by* three

'Did you get his number plate?'

chapter six
going home

'My home,' Stuart said as they pulled up into his driveway a short time later. Much like Adam he also lived in a large detached house on a typical upmarket and well kept estate.

It had been less than a day since he'd last been home but he still felt glad to be back, that was until he jumped out of the car and noticed his front door appeared to have been left open.

'I'm sure I locked it when I left,' he whispered to Cleo as he approached it with caution.

'What are you on about?' she asked following closely behind.

'The door. It's been left open.'

'Are you sure it wasn't just you?'

'I'm sure. I always make sure to lock it,' he said nervously.

three _by_ three

Slowly he pushed the door open with his foot and took a tentative step inside.

Feeling her heartbeat rise uncontrollably Cleo followed behind him.

'Hello,' he shouted down the hall. 'Is anyone here?' he continued although he wasn't sure why. He doubted anyone breaking into his house would be so quick to give themselves, up but he wasn't sure what else he could he do.

'Is anyone else here?' asked Cleo.

'I don't know if they still are, but someone has been,' he replied. 'I'm much tidier than this.' He opened a nearby door and looked into his lounge. It was a mess. Objects were thrown across the floor from one wall to another, but it didn't look as though anything had been stolen, after all, both his laptop and TV were still exactly where he'd left them. Instead, it looked as though someone had been looking for something.

He closed the door and continued up the stairs. Cleo began to follow, but as she walked past a small table in the hallway her attention was caught by a document she spotted on top of it. She picked it up and read the title printed in solid bold lettering across the front;

FLIGHT BV28 - FULL ACCIDENT REPORT

She turned the cover and began reading the first page until;

'I'm sure I left all of these doors closed too,' called Stuart

going home

from upstairs. He didn't speak loudly, but it was enough to make her start and drop the document on the floor.

She picked it up and placed it back on the table before making her way upstairs to join Stuart.

As she reached the top step, she looked around and noticed a small black security camera fixed in place in the corner of the landing. She stared at it, and it stared back at her. A small red light blinked just next to the lens.

'Why do you have cameras fitted? Are they for security?'

'What do you mean?' Stuart replied from within one of the rooms. 'I haven't got any cameras.'

He walked back out onto the landing to see what she was talking about. Noticing the confused look on his face, Cleo pointed up at the camera that continued to watch them. Stuart stared at it, and it stared back at him. The red light continued to blink.

'I didn't put that there,' he whispered under his breath.

Cleo looked back at the camera and then at him. 'Are you sure?'

'I'm sure.'

'Then I'm sorry.'

'Sorry? Sorry for what?' Before he'd a chance to realise what was going on Cleo had taken a step towards him and begun to kiss him. As she did, she glanced up at the camera to make sure that they were both clearly in its view.

Taken aback Stuart pushed her away. 'What are you doing?'

three *by* three

'You need to trust me,' she said hastily. 'Please just trust me. Pack what you need. We need to get away from here quickly.'

'Is there something I should know?'

Cleo looked back up at the camera and wondered if it also recorded sound. While she couldn't have been sure, she decided against taking the risk. Instead, she looked Stuart in the eye and held one of his hands between hers. 'Yes, there is. But not here and not right now. Please just trust me. I know this doesn't make sense, but I need you to trust me.'

He thought for a moment before surprising himself with what he chose to say next. 'Okay, but where do we go?'

'Far away.'

All of a sudden their trail of thought was interrupted as they heard a voice shouting from downstairs. 'Stu? Stuart?'. It belonged to Adam. 'Stuart are you home?' he continued. 'I saw your car outside.'

'He mustn't see you,' whispered Stuart.

'You need to pack quickly then,' Cleo whispered back.

In a quick but quiet and calm panic, Stuart walked into his bedroom and began filling a small travel case with whatever he could find lying about.

He'd just finished zipping up the case when they heard Adam's footsteps on the stairs outside. Holding their breath, they started hoping he wouldn't walk in on them.

Thankfully they heard him walk into a different room and taking their chance they ran out of the bedroom and back

going home

down the stairs.

'So where do we go?' asked Stuart as he threw the case into the back of his car.

'We need to get away from here. But first…'

'…First?' he interrupted.

'I need to go home.'

He looked at her with a clear look of shock on his face. 'I thought you didn't want to go back there?' he asked in disbelief.

'I don't,' she began. 'But there's something I need to get.'

'What?'

'The only thing I've ever had from my father.'

Although every part of him thought it was a ludicrous idea, he knew it was still the right thing to do. 'Where's home?' he asked reluctantly.

It took them little over twenty minutes to drive to the edge of town industrial estate which, despite it being a sunny day, still looked as gloomy as it ever did.

As they began driving further into the estate Stuart began to feel less and less welcome. 'This is the place you call home?' he asked as he sped up while passing a group of hooded teenagers smoking.

'It's the only place I have to call home,' Cleo replied. 'You do get used to the view after a while though. It begins to develop its own unique beauty.'

three *by* three

Stuart sped up again, this time as they passed a couple of lightly dressed women on one of the street corners. 'What about the people? Do you get used to them?'

'The people not so much,' she joked.

'So… which is yours?'

'It's just around the corner up here,' Cleo said pointing out in front of them.

'Is there parking?'

'There's plenty, but it might be best if you didn't use it.'

Agreeing Stuart pulled up at the side of the road and turned off the engine. 'Are you going in alone?' he asked.

'Yes but I need you to come with me anyway.'

'Why?'

'Because I'm not sure getting out again is going to involve using the front door.'

Feeling a mix of confusion and apprehension, Stuart climbed out of the car and followed her around the corner towards the building Cleo called home.

'Aren't they going to see us as soon as the look out the window?'

'I doubt it,' Cleo replied. 'It's impossible to see anything out of those windows.'

'What do you need me to do then?'

'Those over there,' she began, pointing towards some large industrial sized bins that'd been left by the building. 'Make sure one of them is full.'

going home

'What? Why?'

'And then leave it under the end window about a metre out.'

'What are you planning?'

'Just trust me with this.'

'Okay then… anything else?'

'Yes, there is actually. Somewhere around here there should be some gas bottles.'

'Gas bottles? What do you need gas bottles for?'

'I need you to find them and put them all by those gates we've just walked through.'

'Why?' He looked at her with bewilderment plastered on his face although by the look on hers Stuart could only presume she'd already worked out a plan.

'Just put them there and then wait for me out here. I won't be long.'

Stuart stood watching as she walked off into the building before setting about doing what she'd said.

Cleo was surprised to be able to make it all the way to the sixth floor without encountering anyone else, and she considered herself even luckier to find the first room she entered empty.

Although it was quiet, she knew she didn't have long before someone would realise she was back, and so taking her opportunity she made her way across the room to an old cabinet in the corner which she knew had a draw filled with

three *by* three

cash.

While at that point it would've been easier for her to simply walk back out the door without anyone ever knowing she'd been there, she knew there was no way she'd let herself leave without first retrieving the one thing she'd come back for: Not when it was something so important to her.

Cautiously she made her way back out to the corridor and then to the stairs leading to the floor above.

Cleo knew the floorboards on the top floor were known to creek with even the lightest pressure, and so she approached the door to her room with care. When she was just a few steps away though, she heard two voices coming from inside, one of which she recognised to be Ivan's. She stopped and pressed her ear up against the door.

'She's normally back by now,' she heard Ivan say.

'Perhaps she's got into trouble?' a second voice said. 'Caught by the police?'

'It's unlikely. She's too good for the police.' Ivan paused. 'But then it's not impossible. She's been lazy recently and not her usual self.'

'Maybe her preparation hasn't been very good?'

'Her preparation has been fine,' Ivan replied with a subtle hint of anger in his voice. 'I've been preparing her for the past six years.'

'Does she know what for?'

'No. I've always made sure it's kept from her. I doubt we'd

going home

still be able to use her if she knew.'

'Is she not capable?'

'Capable? She's more than capable, that's a certainly,' he said. 'Only, there are some doubts about her mentality.'

'In what way?'

'She has morals, she always has. She might be good when it comes to it but with her it very rarely comes to it. She's always seemed reluctant.'

'What do we do Ivan? Do we find her?'

'No. It's not worth our time to find her. I'm sure we'll find someone else to use.'

'But if she knows things?'

'She doesn't… I've made sure of it.'

'And if she tells someone about this place?'

'Who's she going to tell? She has no one and she is no one. Even if she did tell someone who's going to believe her? She's just a simple girl, a mere homeless girl who is no one. Besides, there're other people looking for her now and they'll be able to deal with her just fine.'

'What do we do with her things?'

'What things?' Ivan said with a laugh. 'She owns nothing.'

Outside the room Cleo jumped as she heard Ivan kicking her bed over and then she froze as: 'What's that,' she heard Ivan say in a suddenly very serious tone.

'Where?' asked the other man.

For a brief second she thought she'd been noticed but she

was safe. 'On the floor,' Ivan continued. She then felt panic again as slowly he asked: 'Is that a book?' He might not have noticed her standing outside but he'd just found her journal and that was something much worse.

She felt her heartbeat rise as she continued to listen.

Inside the room Ivan reached down and picked the tattered journal up of the floor.

'It looks like she's been writing a book,' he joked.

'Perhaps a fairy story where some prince comes to save her and take her away?'

'Well, whatever it is I'm sure she won't mind us having a quick read.'

'Yes I do mind...' she said before could stop herself... Thankfully Ivan was far too busy laughing to hear her.

It wasn't long before Ivan's sense of humour disappeared though as he turned to a random page and began reading what she'd written.

'Ivan...' said the other man noticing the sudden change in expression on his face. 'Ivan, what is it?'

'She knows,' Ivan replied in an almost nervous voice. 'She knows... but how...' He spoke calmly at first but soon began shouting in a rage as he through the journal back onto the floor. 'HOW DOES SHE KNOW?'

'What does she know?'

'We can not wait for someone else to find her, go and find her NOW.'

going home

'Do you want me to bring her back here?'

'No… Just kill her.'

Outside the room Cleo knew she needed to get out of the building as quickly as she could but in her rush to get to the stairs she forgot about the rickety floorboards and a loud creak filled the hallway.

'What was that?' she heard Ivan ask.

She froze and then;

'Oh… Hello,' Ivan said as he stepped out onto the hallway.

Her heartbeat rising further still, she turned to face him.

'Well, it's good to see you make it home safely. When did you get back?' He didn't give her a chance to reply. 'Just now? …'

'Ye…'

'…Just now?' he interrupted, sarcasm returning to his voice. 'Well I'm confused then. If you've only just come back then why do you appear to be on your way back down?'

Not knowing what else to do she turned back and attempted to run for the stairs before suddenly she heard a gunshot and her vision became black as the area around her filled with thick dust.

She presumed Ivan had shot the ceiling above her because she hadn't been hit herself, having already been shot once in the past 24 hours she knew what it felt like.

Beginning to cough, she felt herself being grabbed by the back of her shirt before being thrown forcefully across the hall.

three *by* three

Realising she was now closer to her bedroom door than the stairs she knew there was only one way she'd be able to make it out… she just hoped Stuart had done exactly what she'd told him to.

Cleo crawled her way along the floor into her room just before Ivan pulled her back up to her feet by the neck.

Now in the corner she turned to face him, grabbing (and subtly unlocking) the handle of the nearby.

Looking around the room, she noticed the necklace from her father lying on the floor. More than anything she wanted to reach out and grab it, but at that moment she felt it was more important to concentrate on the gun Ivan was pointing at her.

'Well I think it looks as though a fairytale ending won't be happening this time,' Ivan joked to himself.

'I don't need any man to come and save me,' she said defiantly.

'I can see that.' He leant in to whisper in her ear. 'It's a shame it has to end this way,' he said slowly. 'You were good at what you did.'

He turned to face the other man who was stood watching by the door.

'Could you got fetch something that's a little more… impressive,' he said casually holding up his gun. 'She's family after all.'

The man nodded and left and then;

going home

'WHERE IS SHE?' Ivan shouted out. He'd turned back to face Cleo but instead found himself staring at an empty and dusty corner.

He moved to the door and looked out into the hallways but it was empty, then as he looked back in the room he noticed something... the window was open. In the split second that Ivan had been looking the other way Cleo had climbed out and jumped straight into the bin that Stuart had placed below.

Her plan came as a shock to Stuart who watched in amazement as she appeared from the rubbish.

'You don't mind if I drop in do you?' she said with a smile on her face.

'What just happened? You've just fallen seven floors.'

'There was a reason why I told you to make sure the bin was full.'

Cleo climbed out of the bin just as a bullet was fired from above that only just missing Stuart.

'The gas bottles, did you put them where I told you?' Cleo asked.

'By the gates.'

'Good. We might need to do some running now.'

They continued dodging Ivan's bullets as they made their way back to the gate at the other side of the car park but as Stuart ran through it, Cleo stopped.

'What are you doing?' he shouted back at her in bewilderment as she picked up one of the gas bottles and held

three *by* three

it high above her head.

'Just trust me,' she shouted back.

At that moment the doors to the building smashed open and Ivan's accomplice ran out with his own gun ready to shoot. Both he and Ivan aimed at Cleo and pulled their triggers at the exact time she threw the bottle into the air and ran around the corner to safety.

Less than half a beat later she felt warmth behind her as the two bullets pierced the skin of the bottle and ignited the gas causing the rest of the nearby gas bottles to explode one by one and trap the man chasing them in the car park.

Not stopping to look back she grabbed Stuart's hand and together they ran off back to his car on the next street.

'Does every day with you involve being shot at?' he asked.

'Not every day. Only the exciting ones.'

chapter seven
the two brothers

Eighteen years was a long time. It was possible for a lot to happen in eighteen years.

It was this exact thought that plagued the mind of James Urwin as he sat down to eat lunch in his dressing room on what was likely to be an emotional day for him.

This particular day marked eighteen years since his father had unexpectedly passed away.

Although he was only twelve at the time he died, James had always been able to remember the day vividly in his mind, and on that day, more vividly than ever before.

It started just like any other normal day for him. Attending one of the countries most renowned private schools, normal involved waking up in his dormitory bedroom at around seven in the morning before attending morning prayers and

three *by* three

having breakfast with his friends in the dining hall.

It was soon after that when the day stopped being normal.

Not long after he'd taken his seat at the back of the class for his first lesson of the day, Latin, the headmaster's secretary knocked on the door and walked in asking for him. She said it was important he saw the headmaster right away.

He could remember being led away from the classroom towards the headmaster's study at the other side of the school. At first, he felt glad that he'd been taken out of his least favourite lesson of the week, but as they passed the library, his thoughts turned to worry as he presumed he must be in trouble of some sort, after all, that was why students were usually summoned to see the headmaster. But then he wasn't able to think of anything he could possibly be in trouble for.

When they reached the door of the study, the secretary knocked once before then leading him into the room where he found that his younger brother, Issac, was already sat on a chair in front of the headmaster looking around the room in confusion with worry on his face. Presumably, he also thought he was in trouble for something.

James couldn't help but think it was strange at the time. They might've been related, but he hardly spoke to or even saw his brother, even at home during the holidays.

As he took a seat next to Issac and looked up at the Headmaster, he found himself looking at a face he'd never seen before. He'd seen him angry with students many times but this

the two **brothers**

face wasn't like that, this was a face belonging to a man who'd just received some very bad news.

'I'm very sorry to tell you both this,' the headmaster began. 'But earlier this morning police found your father's car abandoned by a bridge.' James was sure he probably said more at the time but the exact words which were used to tell him he'd never see his father again was the only thing from that day he couldn't recall precisely.

They waited in the Headmaster office for just over an hour until someone came to pick them both up. It was a cold morning, and so the Headmaster himself had gone and prepared them both a hot chocolate in an attempt to make them feel even the smallest amount better.

A short while later a driver from their father's company arrived in one of the big black corporate saloons they used to transport executives around. Usually, both Issac and James were excited to have a chance to ride in these cars, on this occasion however, they felt indifferent. For the entire two-hour journey back to their home James sat in silence and stared out of the window. Issac seemed more confused than sombre, although only being seven he never fully understood exactly what was happening.

When they arrived home, they found their mother sat in silence with two of her husband's business partners who'd come to break the sad news.

Knowing that she'd want to spend some time with her sons

three *by* three

they bid her farewell and left as James and Issac walked in. This wasn't the first time that James had met his father's partners, he 'd seen them many times, and had always got on with them. Both of them had always gone out of their way to talk to him about his interest in science and, in particular, physics. This time however as they passed in the entrance hall of the house they simply patted him on the back with mourning looks on their faces.

Although their father's company was wound up after his death, there was still a fair amount of wealth in it at the time. It was just enough to ensure their mother was able to bring them both up in comfort without having to work and to retain a sizeable sum for both him and his brother for when they were older.

A couple of months later they were removed from their existing school and instead enrolled in another private school much closer to home, although this time, they didn't board. Their mother had always claimed it was because she wanted them to be able to see her every day so she could look after them herself, but James strongly suspected that the same was also true the other way round.

Over the following years, life continued normally, or at least as normally as it possible given the circumstances.

One major difference following their father's death was that James and Issac became much closer to each other. While before they were only brothers by blood the soon became

the two **brothers**

brothers by emotion as well. Their loss had taken a significant toll on both of them, but in the years that followed they bonded and helped each other to grow up in a way that would've made their father proud.

Their mother fell ill shortly before James's 21st birthday and ultimately went on to pass away shortly after it. Just before she had to go into hospital for what'd be the last time though, they'd the chance to go on one last family holiday together.

It was a trip that started well, even despite the overhanging elephant they all managed to enjoy themselves, until one night, halfway through, the mood of the trip changed.

All they'd already been told about how their father had died was that his car was found early one morning by a police officer on his way to work and that they'd never been able to find his body. What they'd never been told however, was what led up to that morning.

With the thought that they were by now old enough to be told and not knowing how much longer she'd be around for, their mother decided to sit them down one evening after dinner and tell them exactly what'd happened.

Although they'd always suspected it, only now were they told for certain that he committed suicide. Their mother however, felt as though they also deserved to know why, and so she then proceeded to tell them about the financial pressure his company had been facing and the personal stress he was also facing too.

three *by* three

At the time the company had just struck a number of new deals with suppliers abroad but when an unexpected recession hit the national economy shortly afterwards, and the value of the currency fell dramatically, the company was no longer able to meet its financial obligations.

Their mother explained how their father had always tried to ensure that the impact the situation had on his workforce was as minimal as possible but no matter what he tried in the coming weeks he knew he'd have no choice but to lay off thousands.

James, who'd always been an intelligent man, understood that while the situation was a tragic one, ultimately there was no one directly responsible for his father's death. After his mother also died he was able to live in peace knowing that they'd both always worked hard throughout their lives and done whatever they could both for their children and those that used to work for them.

After receiving his inheritance James then set about making sure it was used right, and he began investing in projects that'd help create a legacy for both his parents and the Urwin family name.

Issac, on the other hand, took the new information on his father's death in a very different way. There was a part of him that always felt as though his it could've been prevented if only those in the position to prevent the recession had done so. In his mind, the blame needed to rest somewhere, and his belief

the two **brothers**

was that somewhere was with the people who controlled the markets.

After their mother had died Issac had gone on to finish his final two years at school, although he did so as a changed person. Those around him often noted that he seemed much angrier than he ever did before.

James never saw much of Issac over the next few years, although it wasn't through lack of effort. His brother just seemed to become more and more independent and enjoy being alone.

Shortly before Christmas a few years after their mother's death though, his brother turned up unexpectedly at his house one night. After inviting him in they spent some time catching up with the different directions their lives were taking, before Issac told him that he'd decided to go spend some time travelling abroad.

At the time James could only presume Issac had settled down in another country because after that night he didn't see or hear of his brother again for over four years, and that was when they started working together.

Again Issac turned up at his house late one night having just arrived back from Australia a few hours earlier. He said that he'd read about what James was working about online and he finally felt that it was the time for he himself to start working to make his father proud…

three *by* three

...All of a sudden James's trail of thought was broken by a knock on his dressing room door. As he looked around the door opened, and his brother walked in.

Issac was a tall and muscular man with a rough and unshaven face: It was especially noticeable when he was stood next to James who in contrast always made the time to shave every morning.

'Have you been to lay flowers?' James asked.

'Yes, I went this morning. I noticed you've already been?' Issac replied.

'I didn't have the time to go today, so I went last night.'

They were talking about laying flowers for their father. Immediately following his death they'd never had a place to put any as he never had a grave, but after their mother died they began using her's to lay flowers for the both of them.

'How do you feel about today?' Issac asked as he took a seat.

'I'm nervous. It's not an easy presentation to give. There're some big names out there tonight.'

'And they're coming because you're good. This is what you do. You've worked hard for this, nearly ten years of your life has gone into this project.'

'I just hope my speech is good enough.'

'It should be. You've been writing it for over a month.'

'Would you mind checking it a final time for me?'

'Of course. Do you have it now?'

the two **brothers**

'It's in my bag,' James replied. He stood up and walked over to retrieve his bag from the top a sofa in the corner of the room.

As his brother searched for his speech, Issac felt his phone vibrate in his pocket. He pulled it out and read the message on the screen;

SHE KNOWS

He put his phone back into his pocket as James walked back over and handed him a couple of sheets of paper.

'I'll look at it now,' said Issac as he took the paper and began reading his brother's handwriting;

I'd like first to start this evening by dedicating my work on this project to my late father, philanthropist Sir Simon Unwin.

chapter eight
journeying north

Stuart wasn't sure exactly where they were or even how long they'd been travelling for. Ever since they'd left the estate, she'd followed Cleo's instructions just to keep driving North. The events of the past twenty-four hours had left him too tired to pay much attention to any of the towns and cities that kept flashing past in a blur of light.

As he yawned yet another time, he looked across to the passenger seat where Cleo was sat asleep under an old blanket with her head rested up against a makeshift pillow propped up on the window.

He turned his attention back to the road in front. By now it was completely dark and had been for some time. The only light came from the lampposts in the middle of the road and the cars coming the other way.

journeying north

It wasn't long before they passed a flashing sign at the side of the road which made Stuart swear to himself as he read it: the road ahead was closed due to an accident. A short time later they passed another sign, this one advertising not a road closure but a service station only a couple of miles ahead.

He glanced at the clock on the dashboard that'd just clicked over to 8:32 PM and then at his fuel gauge which was now only just above the red line.

Apart from the lunch Cleo had stolen from the garage earlier, neither of them had eaten a thing all day and so unsure when they'd next get a chance he decided it'd be best if they stopped for both for food and fuel.

It was five minutes later when they pulled into an empty parking space outside the service station just as Cleo woke up.

'Where are we?' she asked in a daze.

'Going by the signs, I'd say we're just south of Newcastle.'

'Why have we stopped?'

'We need fuel. I figured you'd probably be quite hungry too.'

'How long have I been asleep for?'

'I'm not sure exactly, maybe five hours,' Stuart replied as he tried to work out exactly how long it'd been since they'd set off.

'I don't think five hours was enough,' she yawned.

'Do you actually have some idea of where we're going?'

'Far away.'

'But far away where exactly?'

three *by* three

'I've already said, just keep driving North.'

'Where are you expecting us to stay? We can't just keep driving: We'll have to stop for the night eventually.'

'I'm sure we'll be able to work that out when we need to.' She looked over at him and smiled. Stuart wasn't sure why but he couldn't help but find her smile reassuring. 'Now,' she continued. 'Did you say there's food nearby?'

It occurred to Stuart, as he climbed out of and locked his car, that he didn't have a way to pay for anything. He hadn't brought any money with him, and all of his cards had been blocked. But, as he found out a few seconds later, it wasn't something he needed to worry about, Cleo had already sorted it.

'Will this cover the fuel?' she asked pulling out a large bundle of notes from her jacket pocket and handing them to him.

'Where…' he began in disbelief. 'Where did you get all this from?'

'It's not easy for criminals to open bank accounts.'

Stuart wasn't sure exactly how much money he now had in his pocket as they made their way through the doors into the warm foyer, but he knew that he certainly had enough for fuel, both for himself and his car.

Even despite the late hour, everything was open, and most places appeared to be busy. The noticeable exception was a small fast food restaurant that would've been entirely empty if it wasn't for the lone waitress sat at a table on her phone with a look of despair on her face.

'There looks good,' said Cleo pointing at a half full cafe that looked as though it had a casual and welcoming atmosphere.

'Okay, we'll go there. I need to go to the toilet first though.'

'I'll order you a coffee.'

'I don't like coffee.'

'Well, I'll just have to drink it for you then.' She smiled at him before walking off to the cafe.

Stuart tried to take as little time as possible in the toilet. Already as he walked in there was a presumably drunken man sat in one of the cubicles babbling about his wife and it wasn't long before he was joined by another who approached him at the sinks to ask if he was interested in buying some questionable looking pills.

While the service station may have had many things the one thing Stuart felt it was lacking was a shoe shop, something he found particularly annoying as he walked out of the toilets feeling as though getting a new and (more importantly) clean pair was a priority.

As he made his way into the café, he found Cleo had chosen a table in the far corner of the room, out of the way of other customers. He sat down opposite her as one of the baristas made their way over to the table carrying two enormous coffees, both of which were topped with generous amounts of cream.

three *by* three

'Which one is mine?' he asked as the barista walked away.

'Oh… neither. You said you didn't like coffee.'

'You could've ordered me something different.'

'I find it difficult to order anything that isn't coffee. It's like an illness. Besides, I couldn't carry anything else.'

'You didn't carry them.'

Cleo simply smiled at him as he stood up. 'Where are you going?'

'I'm going to get myself a tea.'

'Oh, tea… I like tea. Get me one please.'

There was little risk of her tea going cold before she'd a chance to drink it because by the time Stuart returned with them a few minutes later she'd already finished both the coffees.

'You really do like coffee don't you?'

'I haven't had the chance to drink a proper one for a very long time.'

Stuart watched as she took the tea and drank the entire mug in one go. 'You really like tea as well then?'

She nodded. 'Where was that toilet you went to?'

'Just down that corridor.' He pointed across the cafe and out at a small hallway that came off the foyer.

'I'll be back in a minute.'

Stuart continued to watch as she got up and left the café, before nothing a copy of the day's paper that'd been left on the next table by an earlier customer. He reached over to grab it and began reading headline;

PRIME MINISTER CONFIRMS TERROR SUSPICIONS

It was the same paper that Spencer had been reading earlier that morning and like Spencer, Stuart also already knew exactly what the headline was referring to.

As he turned the page, Stuart noticed something out of the corner of his eye. Sat on a table at the other side of the cafe was a man dressed in a plain black suit that made him look as though he was on his way to attend a funeral. Interestingly, Stuart thought, the man didn't appear to have ordered anything, he was just sat on his own at an empty table. He was also sure the man was staring straight at him. Stuart looked over at him, but the man began looking in a different direction, although Stuart was confident he was still watching him in his peripheral vision.

Thinking nothing more of it, Stuart turned his attention back to the paper and he began reading the article on the plane crash until Cleo returned a few minutes later.

'Is that how your parents died?' she asked noticing the headline on the front page. She spoke much more compassionately that before.

'What?' replied Stuart as he looked back at the front page. 'Oh… yeah, it was.'

'I saw the accident report in your house earlier.'

three *by* three

'Accident...' He laughed sarcastically to himself. 'How can it be an accident? A plane doesn't just fall out of the sky for no reason.'

'No... it doesn't.' Cleo paused and thought for a moment. 'It was a bomb.'

'That seems more likely than it being an accident,' Stuart replied casually as he continued to read the article.

'Stuart it was a bomb... I know it was.'

He stopped reading and looked her in the face. 'What do you mean?'

'That flight was brought down by a bomb placed on the plane.'

'How do you know?'

'Because... I know the people who put it there.' She took a deep breath. 'It was the people I lived with.'

'You mean this is what they've been involved with?' he paused and then spoke sounding much more frustrated. 'Why didn't you tell me that earlier? Why didn't you tell me that last night?'

'Because when we were in the forest I didn't know which crash you meant.'

'But what about earlier? What about when you saw the accident report? You must have worked it out?'

'I did. But... but I didn't know how to tell you.'

'You led me to them and you never told me who they were. I could've done something. I could've gone in there and I

journeying north

could've done something.'

'No, you couldn't. I showed you what they've already done to me and you saw how they welcomed me earlier. If you'd have gone in there, you'd have stood no chance. You'd have been shot and killed within a minute.'

'I still could've done something. I could've called the police, called help. They could've been caught there and then. It would've been the end of it.'

'No… it isn't that simple.'

'I don't understand.'

'Yesterday I overheard them talking. There was three of them and they were talking about the crash, they were talking about making sure I'd take the blame for it.'

Stuart glanced down at the photo of the wreckage on the front page and then looked back up at Cleo. 'How do I know they wouldn't be right to?'

'They wanted me to do it at first, but then they decided I wasn't the right person, they thought I'd never be able to do it and so they found someone else.'

'Who were they?'

'I don't know who they got.'

'I mean who were the people you heard talking.'

'I only know one of them. Ivan. He was the one you saw, not the one who ran out but the one in the window. He's the reason my arm looks like it does.'

'Was he the person who planted the bomb?'

three *by* three

'No. I don't think so. I don't think he'd have been able to.'

'Then who did plant it?'

'I don't know.'

'Cleo you need to tell me. My parents died in that crash.'

'I don't know. I've said I don't know.' She spoke in a sudden raised voice, enough to make others in the cafe look over at her and Stuart. 'I'm sorry,' she said talking quietly again. 'I know how this is for you and I wish I could tell you. I've known about it since it happened but I've never known who actually did it and I've never been able to do anything about it.'

'You can do something about it now though.'

'No. I can't. It's still not safe for me.'

'But you're safe. You're with me. They don't know where you are and we can get help together. Look in the paper, they're opening a new investigation, you can go and talk to them, tell them what you know. Not only can you help them but you can help the families of everyone who was on that flight. You can help me.'

'It's not that simple.'

'Then tell me why. Help me to understand.'

'Because this is bigger than that. When I heard them talking yesterday, they didn't sound as though they wanted to make sure I took the blame: they sounded as though they already had.'

'But these investigators don't know about you. They don't know who you are.'

journeying north

'I can't know that for sure.'

'But…'

'I can't…' Cleo interrupted. 'Not yet anyway. I need time to know how to do it right. They wanted that crash to act as a distraction to something bigger. I don't know what that bigger thing is or when it's meant to happen but if I rush to tell someone what I know now then it'll just create even more of a distraction. I don't know how many people are involved with this and I can't rush it, I'll just be playing into their hands if I do.'

'How do I know I can trust you right now?'

Without warning, Cleo leant in across the table and kissed him straight on the lips. 'That's how you can know.'

At that moment Stuart suddenly remembered something from earlier in the day she still hadn't explained. 'Why did you kiss me earlier?' he asked. 'In front of the camera.'

'So that you wouldn't leave me. I want to bring an end to all of this. I want to bring an end to whatever these people are planning, but I know I can't do it alone. I figured that if whoever put that camera there saw us kissing they'd presume we're together and they'd come after both of us. I thought it'd stop you just walking away and forgetting about me.'

'Do you not trust me? Do you really think I'd just walk away from you?'

'I've not had anyone to trust for a very long time. I can't even remember what the word means.'

three *by* three

'Is that why you kissed me just then?'

'No… I kissed you then for a different reason.'

Stuart looked again at the paper. His mind may have been full of thoughts, but at that moment but he knew he was sure, if a little surprised, with his next words. 'You're not going to put a stop to this. We are.'

'You don't have to. You can walk away from all of this.'

'I know I can.' He smiled at her. 'But that doesn't mean that I want to.'

Cleo looked him in the eye as she wiped a tear from her own.

'Right now though there's something much more important we need to sort out,' Stuart continued sounding more lighthearted.

'What's that?'

'Where exactly are we going to stay tonight?'

'Oh… I think I can sort that.'

It was only a minute later when Stuart found himself stood outside one of the service stations many shops staring at a large poster advertising camping equipment. He had to concede, Cleo's ability to think on her feet needed admiring.

'You want to camp?' he asked her, half hoping she was joking.

'No…' She turned to look at him. 'I want both of us to camp.'

'Where exactly?'

journeying north

'I've said. Just keep driving…'

'…North.' He said finishing her sentence.

Neither of them could help but feel surprised, and somewhat relieved, at the range of items the shop sold because twenty minutes later they were packing a large tent, two large blankets, new clothes and some bags of food into the back of Stuart's car. They'd just closed the boot when the suited man ran up to them.

'Excuse me,' he said.

'Yeah?' replied Stuart as he turned his attention to the man.

'You dropped some money as you left the cafe,' the man continued as he handed Stuart a twenty-pound note.

'Oh… thanks.'

'No problem. Have a good evening.'

'You too,' Stuart replied, and with that he watched as the man walked back off back towards the building.

'He's dressed quite formally for a weekend isn't he?' Cleo asked as she climbed into the passenger seat.

'Some people do. Do you remember our old head of year Mr Truslow? He always used to dress in a beige suit, even during the holidays.'

'That reminds me. Do you remember our old Geography teacher?… Miss Jenkins I think her name was.'

'Was she the one who once petitioned the head teacher to ban all forms of kissing and relationships between students?'

'Yeah, that's her. I've seen her around that estate quite a few

three *by* three

times recently… she's a prostitute now.'

It was a noticeably cold Sunday the next day, particularly in the north of Scotland and even more particularly so some thousands of metres above sea level atop the edge of a mountain cliff.

Despite the vigorous and icy winds rustling past the thin walls of their tent both Stuart and Cleo had managed to sleep through most of the night (or at least most of the night that was left after they'd finally decided to make camp).

Neither of them was sure exactly where they were, but they knew it was somewhere in the Scottish Highlands. They'd passed through Edinburgh some time before they stopped.

Stuart was the first to wake, and he walked out of the tent in a still dreamy daze, although it didn't take long for the breeze to wake him up properly.

Taking care not to fall he made his way up to the edge of the cliff and looked down. Between him and the ground was thousands of metres of nothing. He looked back up and out at the view in front of him, unable to help but think just how beautiful it was. For miles and miles, there was nothing more than blue skies and mountain peaks that cast shadows over the small villages that'd been built into the valleys below.

Stuart walked over to his car next to the tent and took out a bottle of water from the boot, before taking a seat on a nearby rock and continuing to admire the view.

journeying north

As he drunk he began considering exactly what the future was now going to hold for him, not that he could actually come up with any ideas, he wasn't even sure what that day would hold for him. There was one thing he was certain of though: He needed to get more answers out of Cleo. She'd been far too vague about what she knew the night before.

After finishing the rest of the water, he threw the empty bottle onto the ground beside him.

'You shouldn't be littering,' he heard a voice say behind him.

He turned to find Cleo stood by the tent. 'How did you sleep?' he asked.

'Not too bad. How about you?'

'I've slept better.'

'Yeah well I've got used to sleeping rough over the years,' she said as she sat down next to him. She tried to put her arm around him, but he pushed it away. 'What's wrong?'

'There's still just too much you haven't told me.'

'What do you mean?' she asked surprised. 'I told you everything you wanted to know last night.'

'You didn't tell me everything. You can't have done. I don't understand how you could've been so involved with these people but not been a part of them bringing the plane down, or how you could never have told anyone it was them.'

'I couldn't have done. They'd have killed me.'

In the corner of his eye, Stuart noticed her beginning to

pull her sleeve up. 'You don't need to show me your arm again.'

'You've seen what they've already done to me. I couldn't have told anyone.'

'Then why did you tell me?'

'Because… I trust you.'

'And how do I know I can trust you?'

'You can't. There isn't a way. But if you don't then why did you come with me?'

'I really don't know.' He stood up and walked back over to his car.

'Stuart?'

'I just need some time to clear my head and think about things.'

'Where are you going?'

'That village we passed through last night. I'm going to get some more food.'

'Are you coming back?'

'Yes, soon. I promise. I just need some time.'

Cleo stood up and ran over to him as she pulled some more money out of her pocket. 'Use this,' she said handing it to him. 'Get something for breakfast. I'll get a fire started.'

'Thanks.'

The drive back down the mountain road only took ten minutes but nevertheless it was a drive that made Stuart wonder exactly how they'd survived driving up it the night before. Even in daylight it was a difficult road to drive on.

journeying north

Stuart never noticed the name of the village when they'd gone through it during the night, but as he drove past the first set of houses he noticed a large sign set in stone that read: 'Welcome to Braemar'.

It was only a small village, but it was one that was full of tradition and character, and no matter which direction he looked in, he was always able to spot a traditional Highland touch. While the number of houses making up the village wasn't particularly large, no two of them were the same: all were in some way different and unique.

Stuart parked close to a small campsite at the other end of the village, and after locking his car, he set off on foot to a small café that he'd noticed while driving through.

Although it wasn't a fashionable or especially upmarket cafe it was full of time-honoured Scottish quirks, from the tartan carpet to the matching tartan patterned table cloths. Along one side of the room was a large (and currently unlit) open fire while opposite it was a counter display of homemade cake slices and of course, shortbread.

Stood behind the counter but in front of a large poster from several decades ago advertising Irn Bru was a friendly woman in her later 50's. As Stuart entered the café she walked over to him and introduced herself as Rachael, the café's owner. After showing him to an empty table, she took his order for a fresh cup of tea and a slice of her highly recommended shortbread. It may still have been time for

three *by* three

breakfast, but Stuart felt he was tired enough to justify something sugary.

Soon after he'd finished his first cup of tea and ordered a second another customer walked into the cafe. Like Stuart, he was also greeted gleefully by the café's owner and shown to another empty table before she took his order for a single glass of still water.

As Stuart looked over at the man he noticed something very peculiar about him: He was dressed in a full black suit... on a Sunday. Not only that but as he looked at his face Stuart was sure that he'd seen it before, he was sure that it was the same man he'd seen at the service station, the same man who'd run out to give him the money he'd dropped. But it couldn't be him Stuart thought to himself. They were now hundreds of miles away from the service station, and there was no way anyone could've followed them that far.

Stuart didn't get too much time to dwell on the thoughts, as Rachael had just returned with his tea. 'Can I get you anything else?' she asked.

'Do you have a newspaper?'

'Of course I do. I'll just get it for you in a moment.'

Stuart watched as she disappeared into the kitchen before returning no more than a minute later with a glass of water for the suited man, and the morning paper for him.

'There you go,' she said handing it to him.

'Thank you.'

journeying north

'So what brings you up to Scotland then?' she asked. 'Your accent doesn't sound like you're from here.'

'No, I'm not. I live in London. I'm just up here for...' he stopped as he thought about the best way to continue. 'I'm just up here for some time off work.'

'Just needed a break from the city life?'

'Yeah.'

'I understand the feeling. I've got two daughters who both work down in London. They love the city, but they never fail to look forward to coming home every few months for a break. I've always preferred the country myself. I find the city to be far too formal.' She leant in and gestured towards the suited man. 'Although it looks as though some people enjoy formal a bit too much.'

Stuart, trying to be polite, laughed along with her until he was able to turn his attention to the paper after she'd walked back to the kitchen.

There wasn't anything of much interest on the first few pages, but then this wasn't his usual paper. This one seemed to be much more interested in making every headline football related rather than reporting the actual news. It wasn't until he reached page 14 that he finally found something that was worth reading;

PHOTO RELEASED OF PLANE CRASH SUSPECT

three *by* three

He'd often seen headlines relating to the crash over the past year, but this one was different. This was the first time he'd seen one that both openly revealed the possibility of the crash not being an accident and said who may have been responsible for downing it. With keen interest, he began to read the accompanying article;

The Independent Security Service tasked with undertaking a new investigation into the loss of flight BV28 on direct orders from the Prime Minister following the discovery of new evidence, has this morning released a photograph of an individual they suspect may have been behind the sabotaging of the fight. Although formal identification of the individual is yet to take place.

… Stuart stopped reading. He'd just noticed who's photo was printed next to the text. It was the person who he'd been trusting. It was the person he'd been helping to escape… It was Cleo.

Without a second thought, he stood up and ran out of the café back to his car. He wasn't sure precisely what he was going to do when he got there, but he knew he needed to get back up the mountain as quickly as possible.

On his return, he found Cleo sat on a rock warming her hands on the small fire she'd started. As he pulled up and climbed out of the car, she didn't notice the look of anger on his face. 'I'm glad you're back. I'm getting hungry,' she said.

journeying north

Stuart didn't respond. Instead, he simply thrust the paper into her gaze.

'What's this?' she asked looking up at him.

'You lied to me.'

'What do you mean?'

'You lied to me... it's in the paper. It was you who brought that plane down. It was you who killed my parents.'

'Stuart I've told you, I had no...' She stopped as she noticed her own face staring back at her from the paper. Taking it from his hand, she began reading what it said beside the photo. 'This... this isn't true,' she said looking back up at him. 'I don't understand it.'

'Well, I do. It's clear. It was you.'

'Listen to me,' she said as she stood up. 'I was never involved with that crash. I couldn't have been. I'm not that sort of a person.'

'But you are the sort of person to chase people through a forest armed with an axe though.'

'I was forced to... I couldn't just walk away.'

'How do I know that? How do I know you didn't do it by choice? Of course you could've walked away if you'd have wanted to, you walked away with me yesterday.'

'That's different.'

'Why is it different?'

'Because I trust you. I thought you'd be my way to a normal life.'

three *by* three

'I think you thought wrong.'

'If I thought wrong then why are you still here?' She said, not realising what she was saying until it was too late to stop herself.

'Because I thought I could trust you. But I was wrong.'

'Stuart...' She took a step towards him but he ignored her. She watched as he walked back over to his car. 'Stuart what are you doing?' Still he ignored her as he climbed into the driver's seat and turned on the engine. 'Stuart,' she shouted. 'You can't leave me up here.' It was hopeless. He either couldn't hear her or he was choosing not to. All she could do was stand and watch as he drove off, this time unsure if he'd be coming back.

Stuart was angry, although he wasn't sure if he was angry with Cleo or himself for leaving her. Regardless of what he might have seen in the paper, there was still a large part of him that simply couldn't believe that she'd be involved with such a plot.

He wasn't sure where else to go, and so he decided first to return to the café. As he walked back in the first thing he noticed was that the suited man was still there. He sat down at the same table as before, just as Rachael appeared from the kitchen.

'Oh,' she said walking up to him. 'I'd wondered where you'd gone in such a hurry.'

'I had...' He knew he had to think quickly. 'I had to get something from my car.'

journeying north

'Can I get you another tea?

'Please.'

As she walked back off to the kitchen Stuart couldn't resist the urge to let his face fall into his arms on the table. He sat for a while in deep thought, until;

'Mr Wright?' he heard a man's voice say.

He looked up at the man stood in front of him.

'Zachary Jones,' continued the man as he held out his ID. 'I work for the Independent Security Service. Do you mind if I take a seat?'

Stuart nodded. He knew he didn't really have a choice.

'Thank you,' said Zachary as he pulled himself up a chair. Stuart watched as he nodded towards the suited man. As she did the man stood up and walked out of the café to stand just outside the front door. 'Don't worry,' Zachary said as he noticed Stuart watching him. 'He works for me. He's just going to make sure that we're not distributed.'

'I saw him yesterday. He was watching me in a service station.'

'Yes, that would've been him. We've been following you up here. That note he gave you yesterday, it had a small tracker on it. We needed to make sure that you weren't in any danger before we spoke to you alone.'

'What do you mean danger?'

Zachary reached in his jacket pocket and pulled out a small photograph of Cleo before placing it on the table in front of

three *by* three

Stuart. 'I believe you know this girl?'

'Is that what you want to talk to me about?'

'Can you tell me what you know about her?'

'She's just an ordinary girl.'

'Can you tell me where she lives?'

'I...' He paused, a part of him was unsure if he should be honest or not. 'She never said.'

'What's your personal relationship with her?'

'We went to the same school. We shared classes together.'

'Can you tell me what your relationship with her is now?'

'I don't understand?'

'Are you friends? More than friends? Accomplices?'

'I don't know. I hadn't seen her for six years until Friday when...' he stopped again.

'Yes, Mr Wright?'

'We met again.'

'And what were the circumstances around that reunion?'

'Don't you already know that?'

'I know you carried her to your car and spent the night sleeping in it. I followed you on CCTV that night. What I want to know is how you got to that situation in the first place. You do have your own home don't you? Why didn't you take her back there? Where did you carry her from?'

Stuart didn't respond. Instead, he watched as Zachary reached back into his pocket and pulled out another photo. This too was a photo of Cleo, but this time she was with someone else, someone Stuart immediately recognised to be him.

He leant forward to look at it more closely and noticed that it appeared to be taken from the camera he'd seen in his house the previous day. 'You're the people who put the camera in my home?'

'Yes, that was us. It's part of our job. Can you please explain this photo for me?'

He looked down at it again and noticed it seemed to show both him and Cleo kissing each other. 'It's just a photo,' he said looking back up at Zachary.

'Can you explain why you appear to be kissing each other? It seems highly unlikely to me that two people who'd just happened to reunite for no particular reason would feel comfortable being that close together.'

'There wasn't a reason for it. I wasn't expecting it, she just moved in and did it.'

'Do you know why?'

'I didn't at the time, but last night she said it was so I wouldn't leave her.'

'Mr Wright I'm sorry to tell you this, but this girl is a terrorist.'

Stuart fell silent. Even with what he was hearing now and everything that he'd seen in the paper he still didn't know what to believe. Cleo had simply never in his mind seemed that sort of a person.

three *by* three

Sensing his thoughts Zachary reached over to a nearby table and grabbed the paper that'd been left on top of it. 'I presume you've seen today's paper? he asked as he opened it to the page about Cleo.

'How can she be? She's not that person.'

'Some people are talented at appearing to be different from the person they truly are.'

'Why would she have done it? She has no reason to want to bring a plane down, and she certainly wouldn't know how to.'

'Oh she had help to do it, and she had plenty of to as well. We believe it was done to act as a distraction away from something else she's planning. We don't know what it is yet, but we believe that she wants to involve you so that she can avoid taking the blame herself.'

'That's what she said other people were doing to her. She said the people she was living with were trying to force her to do things that she didn't want to do. She said they were the ones who wanted to use it as a distraction and that they were trying to make sure she'd take the blame for it.'

'Did she tell you anything about who these people were? Did she say what they were trying to distract from?'

'No. She said she'd written it all down though.'

'We've searched the building she was living in, but we didn't find anyone else living there. The only thing we did find was an old journal that she's been writing in.'

'She said she overheard a conversation on Friday.'

journeying north

Zachary suddenly felt his mouth go very dry. 'Yes?' he pressed.

'She said she'd heard three people talking about her and about the crash. She said she'd heard one of them saying they were already ensuring that it was a distraction.'

'Did… did she say who she'd overheard?'

'She only knew one of them, but she said she saw the other two and wrote.'

Zachary swallowed hard before continuing. 'That man out there,' he said gesturing towards the door. 'He said he overheard you both talking about doing something together last night. Can you elaborate on that for me please?'

'She told me she knew who'd brought the plane down but she'd never been able to do anything about it. She was worried about what could happen to her. So I promised her I'd help her do something.'

'Mr Wright can you tell me what her name is?'

'It's Cleo… but surely you already know that?'

'Can you tell me her full name?'

'Cleo…' he thought, but nothing came to him. 'Cleo… I… I can't remember her surname.'

'You can't remember her name?… You've let her travel with you, and you've believed everything she's told you but you don't even know what her name is?'

'I just… I trusted her.'

'You trusted wrong. She's the reason you don't have your

parents right now. She's the reason you don't have any family left.'

'I still don't understand how it could be her?'

'You don't need to understand it. You need to accept it. She's been playing you along so she can make sure you're the one who takes the blame while she walks off.'

'What am I meant to do?'

'Personally I don't believe you had any involvement with bringing that plane down. We've been following her for months but you never appeared until Friday. You'll be free to go today, but I need you to make a formal statement first.'

'What about Cleo? What's going to happen to her?'

'We know where she is and we've got people who are going up there as we speak.'

'What about after that though? Will she be okay?'

'Will she be okay? Mr Wright she's a terrorist. She was behind one of the biggest acts in this countries history. It's not her that you should be worrying about, it's people like yourself, the families of her victims.'

'I know... I just can't help but care... I thought...'

'... It's wasted,' Zachary interrupted. 'Whatever you think of her she doesn't think the same about you. She's just good at acting.'

'What happens next?'

'My team have set up a small monitoring centre down the road from here. I'll take you there to give your statement and then you'll be free to go. After that, it'd probably be best if you just chose to forget about all of this and, more importantly, if you opted to forget about her too.'

Stuart gazed out of the café window in thought before eventually swallowing hard and nodding.

It only took them a few minutes to walk to what Zachary had referred to as a monitoring centre. Personally, Stuart couldn't help but think that it looked much more like a large garden gazebo filled with expensive looking computers pitched next to seven jet black 4x4s.

As they walked by one of the cars, Zachary turned to Stuart. 'Please take a seat for a moment, Mr Wright,' he said pointing towards two plastic chairs that were next to the car.

Stuart did as he was asked and then watched as Zachary walked over to two suited men stood by one of the other cars.

'The journal that was found,' Zachary whispered to them. 'I need you to make sure that it's locked in my office as soon as possible.'

'Yes sir,' said the men together.

Stuart couldn't help but wonder precisely what Zachary was doing as he then watched him walk into the tent before returning a few minutes later with another suited man by his side.

'Mr Wright,' Zachary said as he walked back over to him. 'This is Elliot. He's just waiting for his colleague and then they're going to escort you to a nearby hotel so you can make

three *by* three

your statement and have a chance to eat and shower before you go back down to London.'

He wasn't exactly sure why but Stuart couldn't help but feel uneasy and suspicious as he climbed into the back of one of the cars while Elliot climbed into the front. After a short wait, yet another suited individual climbed into the passenger seat and they set off towards the main road and then out of the village.

It wasn't long before Stuart began to think he may have been right to feel suspicious when the car pulled up in a lay-by just a few miles outside the village.

'Elliot isn't it?' he said. 'What's going on? Have we broken down?'

Elliot didn't reply: he simply turned off the engine.

Stuart looked up at the rearview mirror and noticed him reaching into in inside pocket.

The next few moments happened quickly. Within seconds Stuart went from watching Elliot pull out a gun from his jacket pocket and aim it directly at him, to watching Elliot then fall into an unconscious slump in his seat as the car's other passenger jabbed something hard into his arm.

Stuart looked briefly at Elliot before then turning his attention to the person who seemed to have just saved his life.

'I think you owe me a thank you,' said Cleo.

'What are you doing? You've killed him.'

'No... He's not dead,' she replied as she pulled a small

syringe and needle out of Elliot's arm. 'He's just... sedated. I found these things lying around their tent. He'll be okay soon enough.'

'What are you doing here?'

'I figured you'd be interested in not being murdered today.'

'Cleo you can't do this. You need to hand yourself in.'

'Listen to me. I didn't bring that plane down. How could I have? I'm just a young girl. I don't know how to get past airport security undetected.'

'But these people. They're the security services. They know you did it. They told me you did it.'

'Did they actually show you any evidence?'

'No... but the evidence is going to be classified.'

'What else did they tell you?'

'They said you wanted to try to blame me for it and that's why you tried to make it look as though we were together.'

'And what else? Did they say you'd be free just to walk away?'

'They said they wanted me to make a statement first but then, yes, after that I'd be free.'

'And how exactly is that working out for you? I may not be an expert but I didn't think freedom involved being parked in the middle of nowhere while someone shoots you in the head.'

'What are you expecting me to do? Who do you expect me to trust?'

'I don't expect you to know but consider this, they're the

ones who just tried to kill you and I'm the one who just saved your life.' Cleo turned her attention away from Stuart and opened the car door.

'Where are you going?'

'I'm going to get us out of here.'

'You can't. You need to hand yourself in, if you're innocent then prove it to them and you'll be free to go.'

Cleo ignored him and made her way around to the other side of the car to open the driver's door before pulling the unconscious body of Elliot out onto the ground below with little care for his wellbeing. Once he was safely out of the way she climbed into the driver's seat and turned the engine back on.

'What are you doing?' Stuart asked in a panic. 'You can't drive can you?'

'I don't think I actually know the answer to that… I'll just have to let you judge for yourself.'

Even before he'd finished taking his next breath, Stuart felt himself being forced back hard into his seat as Cleo put her foot down on the accelerator and set off back towards the village at speed.

A few short minutes later they' reached the bottom of the mountain they'd been camping on, and Cleo slowed down as they began climbing the mountain road. 'We're going to need to go back up and get some things. We won't stand a chance if we run unprepared.'

journeying north

'Run? I'm not doing any more running. I've had enough of this now.'

Cleo didn't say anything else until they reached their campsite half way up the mountain, when she turned the engine back off and then turned to Stuart.

'You need to trust me, right now even more than you've done over the past few days. I know I'm asking a lot from you but I need you to know that I didn't bring that plane down but I do know who did and I can do something about it. You've shown me that I can do something about it, but I'm going to need your help to do it.'

'Then hand yourself in and prove that you're innocent. We can end this today.'

'They said you were free to go and then they tried to kill you. Do you think they'd even give me a chance to introduce myself when they already think I'm guilty?'

'How do I know I can trust you?'

'I can't make you trust me. But I trust you.'

Stuart stopped and thought for a moment, something that couldn't help but make Cleo feel more and more anxious as each second passed. Eventually, he looked her in the face and smiled. 'I presume you can sort this?'

'With your help… yes.'

'Okay. What do we do?'

'We go back down the mountain.'

'Why have you just driven up it then?'

three *by* three

'Because we need to go back down to London and to do that we're going to need money,' she replied climbing out the car and beginning to take off the suit she was wearing over her other clothes. 'If I'm right they should also be following us up here right about now... and yes... they do appear to be doing that,' she added as she looked down the mountain road.

Stuart also climbed out the car and looked down at the approaching convoy of black 4x4s that Cleo was pointing at.

'I'd say we've about three minutes,' she said not sounding at all concerned.

'Three minutes until what?'

'Until they get up here and we need need to be gone.'

'How are we going to get back down though? They're blocking the road.'

'Just get what we need from the tent and your car.'

Stuart thought it best not to press her further. If the previous day had taught him anything, it was that she'd already planned out exactly what they were going to do next. Opening the boot of his car he grabbed a rucksack and began filling it with everything he thought they'd need including a change of clothes both of them, and, more importantly, the rest of their money.

'I'm ready,' he said walking back over to Cleo who was busy looking through the boot of the other car.

'Good. Now put this on,' she said handing him a large bag.

'What is it?'

journeying north

'A parachute.'

'A parachute? Why do I need a parachute?'

'Well we can always share if you really want to,' she replied as she began clipping another around her waist.

'Did you know they were in there?'

'No... no, I didn't. I was just hoping that something useful would be.' Noticing him struggling with his own she approached Stuart to help him tighten the parachute's straps. 'Right, I think that's about right... are you ready?' she continued sounding much more excited than she did nervous.

'I'm... I'm actually really not so quite sure about this I think,' he blurted out sounding much more nervous than he did excited.

'It's going to be a lot safer than trying to pass the convoy of cars that's currently...' she glanced back down the mountain road. '...I'd say about 40 seconds away.'

'Hold on... Just hold on for a moment.'

'We haven't got time. We need to jump now.'

'But there's still something I want to know first.'

'This really isn't the right time.'

'It's just one quick thing.'

'I've already told you everything you wanted to know.'

'It's not about that.'

'What is it about then?'

'Why did you want to come up to Scotland?'

'Oh... I once saw a picture of the place and thought it

three *by* three

looked nice.'

Hearing engines fast approaching Stuart glanced back down the road. He looked back expecting to see Cleo but she'd already jumped. With no other option, he took a run up to the edge of the cliff and jumped.

Seconds later he began wishing he had a pen and paper to note down some of the swear words he'd just invented for future use.

Below him the ground fast approaching seemed to be looking more and more solid as each moment passed, and then, instinctively, he pulled the cord to release the parachute and shot back up into the air before beginning to glide gently downwards.

Looking over at Cleo he noticed that apart from looking happier than ever she also seemed to be aiming to land on a specific grassy area just outside the village.

Slowly his confidence in the parachute increased and he was soon able to start enjoying the view as he descended. So much so that by the time his feet hit the ground he was almost disappointed the experience was over.

'Can I just say,' Cleo began as she untangled herself from her parachute. 'That was much more comfortable than jumping out of a window into a bin was yesterday.'

'I actually think I want to try that again,' Stuart replied breathlessly. 'But what do we do now? We've left our transport half way up a mountain and we're in the middle of the

journeying north

Highlands.'

'Didn't you look for anything on the way down?'

'I was too busy admiring the view.'

'Are you referring to the mountains or me?'

Stuart couldn't help but smile to himself. 'I presume you noticed something then?'

'They left a car behind.'

'Won't they have someone guarding it?'

'Didn't you see how many of them followed us up there? They weren't expecting us to make it down before them. Trust me: that car will be free for us just to walk up and take.'

By now Cleo was starting to build up an impressive run of being right about things, because sure enough after they made she short walk from where they'd landed they found one of the jet back 4x4s sat waiting for them, and with no one else around it wasn't long before they found the keys and on were their way out of the village.

It was late afternoon by the time they next stopped. They were in another small Scottish village but they weren't sure exactly which one. While they'd been hoping to find a station so they could get back to London as quick as possible, they'd also been eager to frequently change direction to make it harder for anyone to follow them.

'Stuart we've found one,' Cleo said as she parked up in the small car park outside the station.

three *by* three

Although he wasn't completely asleep, Stuart was starting to feel drowsy from exhaustion and he hadn't been paying much attention to anything for the past few hours. 'Which one is it?' he said in a daze.

'Hold on… Blair Atholl,' she said reading from a sign she could see at the other side of the car park. 'It doesn't look like a busy one though.'

'We might have quite a wait for the next train then. What time is it?'

Cleo glanced at the clock on the dashboard in front of her. 'Half four.'

'I just hope we haven't missed the last one of the day.'

After spending a short time stretching and enjoying the fresh air they set about raiding the car for anything they thought might come in useful (including personal protection). A little while later, and after they'd packed what they needed into Stuart's rucksack, they made their way over to the ticket office at the other side of the car park.

'Excuse me,' said Stuart as he approached the man sat behind the desk.

'Yes sir,' the man replied in a strong Scottish accent. 'How can I assist this afternoon?'

'Can you tell us when the next train to London is please?'

'London?… Well, you've missed the direct one, that left about an hour ago and I don't think there're any connections available at this time either. Hold on a moment for me please,'

journeying north

said the man as he began typing something into the computer in front of him. 'There's an overnight sleeper service that arrives into Euston at about seven tomorrow morning. It doesn't leave here until just past ten this evening though.'

Stuart looked over to Cleo. She nodded at him. They both knew it was their best option. 'That'll be fine,' Stuart said as he turned his attention back to the ticket man.

'Is it just the two of you?'

'Yeah, just us two.'

'Okay, that'll be a total of £450 then please.'

Although they felt surprised at the cost, they could tell from his face that the ticket man felt even more surprised to watch Stuart pull a large bag of money out of his pocket and pay the entire amount in cash.

It took him a while for the man to count out all of the notes, but after a few minutes, he finally handed them two pieces of paper. 'And here are your tickets. It'll be platform one. There's a waiting room on the platform but it's not very good. I'd recommend going to the pub that's just around the corner for a few hours. They do some good food in there and I think they offer some showers too.'

'Thank you,' Stuart replied. 'We'll go there for a while then. What time is the train?'

'It departs at five past ten but it usually arrives here around five minutes early.'

After thanking him one final time they left the ticket office and began making their way back across the car park.

'You know,' said Cleo. 'I think I actually quite like Scotland.'

'Is it me or did he just suggest I need to take a shower?'

'Well if he didn't, I am now.'

'Why?'

'Because you stink.'

end of the line

It wasn't the constant racketing sound of the old carriages shaking their way along the tracks but rather the bright sun shining through the old nylon curtain in front of their cabin window and onto his face that woke Stuart the next morning.

As he sat up in his bed, he yawned and looked across at Cleo who was still asleep on the next bed. He didn't think there was a need to wake her just yet: they were still some distance away from London, and he knew she'd be tired. Unsure when they'd next get a chance to eat, he instead decided to go in search of breakfast.

He reached over to his jacket that was hung on the back of the door and rummaged through his pockets until he found a scrunched up ten-pound note. After then taking a few moments to stretch he set off towards the restaurant car in the

three by three

middle of the train.

As he walked through the vestibule into the carriage, he found it to be around half full with a small number of people queuing for the buffet. He looked up at the clock on the wall that'd just ticked over to half six. He felt surprised to have been able to sleep for so long with so much on his mind.

He joined the back of the queue and after a short wait was able to purchase two hot bacon sandwiches (with extra bacon), and a copy of that morning's paper before he made his way back to his cabin.

On his return, he found Cleo awake and busy cleaning the gunshot wound on her arm from Friday.

'Is it still hurting?' Stuart asked as he sat down on his bed.

'It stings,' she replied. 'I can't do anything but wait for it to heal itself though. I'm not sure I could explain how it happened to a doctor.'

Stuart threw her one of the sandwiches which she caught with her other, non-injured, arm.

'What's this?' she asked.

'It's bacon.'

'Did I ever tell you I used to be a vegetarian?'

'Are you still?'

He didn't hear her response. Instead, he watched it as she took the sandwich from peaceful foil wrapping, and, in a single bite, ate nearly half of it at once. With her mouth full she looked him in the face and attempted a smile. 'How long until we arrive?' she asked taking another (this time smaller) bite.

'We've got about half an hour,' Stuart said as he began to unwrap his own sandwich.

'I best go freshen myself up then.' And with that, she left the cabin with a spare set of clothes in one hand and the remainder of her breakfast in the other.

Stuart watched her leave before turning his attention to the day's paper.

He couldn't help but feel surprised when he read the word Monday at the top of the page. The weekend had been such a blur to him that he'd rather lost track of the days. Usually at this time on a Monday morning, he'd be stuck in the early rush hour traffic on his way to his central London office. While it was still true he was on his way to London that morning, it just wasn't to spend a day behind his desk. Even despite the circumstance however, Stuart still felt as though it was already one of the best Monday mornings he'd ever had.

As he began surveying the front page his attention was drawn to the headline;

INVENTOR SOLVES WORLD FUEL CRISIS

He looked at the photo under the headline. It was of a man holding up a small device that was no bigger than his own hand. Intrigued Stuart began to read the accompanying article;

three *by* three

James Urwin, son of former business tycoon Sir Simon Urwin, revealed at an exclusive event on Saturday evening, his latest invention which he claims is the solution to the world's ongoing fuel crisis.

During a keynote presentation Mr Urwin stated that while many individuals don't see the world as having a problem with energy creation during their everyday lives, it's an issue which should be dealt with sooner rather than later.

His invention, a device he calls a Hydrogen Cell, is claimed to provide enough energy to power a single house for up to 3 months. It was explained that the device works by storing compressed hydrogen gas in solid form before turning that gas into energy using a micro generator built into the device.

Despite some concerns raised by physicists around the country regarding the safety of such a device, particularly in relation to the storage that gas in such a form, Mr Urwin announced that a total 2500 devices are to be rolled out to councils across London, starting today.

Also speaking at the event was the inventor's brother, Issac Urwin who announced that a smaller version of the device in a battery form will also be handed out free to commuters across London later this week.

Stuart was concentrating so hard on the article that he didn't notice Cleo had returned until his view of the paper was suddenly blocked by the cup of coffee she held in front of it.

end of the line

He looked up at her.

'You'll need it,' she said. 'It's probably going to be another long day.'

'I thought I told you I don't like coffee?'

'Do you still?'

She began laughing as he put the paper to one side before proceeding to drink the entire cup in one go.

'So, do you have any plan for today?' she asked sitting down next to him.

'Do you?' he replied.

'No.'

'No. Neither do I. We're probably going to need to find somewhere to stay first though, but we don't have much money left, and I'm almost certain that going home wouldn't be a good idea.'

'Where do we go then?'

'The Pacific Islands look Finally,,' he joked as he drew her attention to an advert for a South Pacific cruise that was in the paper.

'It looks beautiful.'

'I'm sure with you there it would be,' he said, feeling almost immediately embarrassed. Cleo smiled subtly to herself as Stuart then turned his attention to the view outside the window in an attempt to hide the look on his face.

A short time later their train slowed and pulled into its final station, London Euston.

three *by* three

It'd only just turned half seven, but despite the early hour, the station was already bustling with busy commuters making their way from the platforms towards the exit and underground station with varying levels of enthusiasm for their days ahead.

Inside their cabin, Stuart and Cleo were busy clearing up and repacking their things, which now included a gun and Fetch smoke grenades that they'd been able to take from the stolen car the day before.

As Cleo held the gun in her hand, there was an unexpected knock on their cabin door. Stuart waited while she made sure it was out of view before opening the door.

'Good morning Mr Wright.' It was one of the trains hosts. 'Your driver is waiting for you out on the platform.'

'Okay... thanks...' Stuart replied feeling perplexed.

'Shall I tell them that you're on your way?' asked the host.

'No.. It'll be okay thanks.'

'Okay sir. Do have a good day.'

'I don't remember you giving them your name when we got on,' Cleo said as the host walked back off down the carriage.

'That's because I didn't.'

Cleo stood back as Stuart took a step forward into the corridor of the carriage and bent down to look through the window at the platform outside. Stood in a single straight line were six men all dressed in solid black suits and, at the end of the line, Zachary.

end of the line

Hastily Stuart made a retreat into the cabin and closed the door, making sure to also pull down the curtain to stop anyone from looking in.

'What is it?' asked Cleo noticing the look on his face.

'They've followed us,' he said. 'We're going to need to move fast.' Stuart looked down at the bed and realised they were still far off being packed. 'We'll have to leave most of this stuff. Just grab what you need.'

Quickly they both moved to sort through what they thought they'd most need, and a minute later they were ready.

Stuart pulled back the curtain and looked into the corridor: it was still empty. Making the most of the time they still had he grabbed a bag from the bed and began filling it with bits of rubbish that were lying around the cabin before also adding one of the smoke grenades.

'What are you doing?' Cleo questioned.

'I'm going to try to give us as much time as possible.'

Out on the platform Zachary was now stood by the door to their carriage with one of the suited men by his side. 'Find them,' he instructed the man.

Inside their cabin, Stuart and Cleo could hear someone approaching. They started as they heard a loud crash as one of the cabin doors at the other end of the carriage was kicked open, followed a brief time later by another, and another, each time getting closer to theirs.

Cleo reached for the gun and got in position to aim at the

three *by* three

door.

'Don't shoot anyone,' whispered Stuart as he pushed her arm back down.

They looked up at the door just as a silhouette appeared at the other side, and then, seconds later, they found themselves face to face with the suited man.

Stuart stared into his eyes before all of a sudden, and for no apparent reason, the man fell to the ground.

'What happened?' Stuart asked as turned to look at Cleo who was now holding an emergency exit hammer in her hand.

'You told me not to shoot.'

Feeling both impressed with Cleo and slightly sorry for the man he looked down at the ever-growing pool of blood at his feet coming from the side of the man's head. 'You've ruined the carpet.'

'It looks as though I may have done that yes.'

'I think we should probably go now.'

Knowing they wouldn't stand a chance if they came out onto the platform Cleo moved over to the outside window and struck it once in the corner with the hammer. Instantly the glass went from transparent to opaque as it cracked all the way from one corner to the other. She then grabbed a nearby pillow from the bed and used it to push outwards on the window, making it shatter and fall out onto the next track.

Making sure not to cut herself on any of the sharp edges left around the frame she climbed up and out onto the track,

end of the line

followed shortly afterwards by Stuart.

They crossed the rails and threw their bags up on the opposite platform. Cleo had no problem with pulling herself up too, but as she looked back around she noticed Stuart unable to do so the same.

She looked down the platform and noticed another train pulling into the station on the same track. 'Stuart move quickly,' she shouted at him.

By now Zachary had also boarded their train himself and made his way to their cabin.

Cleo looked up and noticed him getting ready to shoot at Stuart, and then, without realising, she instinctively reached into her pocket, pulled out a gun and shot at Zachary.

Although she was some distance off actually hitting him, it was enough to ruin his aim.

Noticing Zachary needed to reload she ran forwards to the edge of the platform and reached down to give Stuart a hand up. With her help, he managed to make it up onto the platform just breaths before the arriving train passed.

Taking no time to catch their breath, they mingled with the crowd that was now pouring off the newly arrived train and began making their way towards the station concourse.

In their rush to leave the train, they'd both misplaced their tickets. Thankfully though the crowd was large enough for them to slip past the ticket inspectors at the end of the platform with relative ease.

three *by* three

'Hold on,' said Stuart as suddenly he stopped walking.

'What?' Cleo replied as she looked back at him. 'Stuart we can't waste time, we need to go.'

'I've got an idea.' She watched as he reached into the bag he was carrying to retrieve the smoke grenade. He then pulled the pin out of the grenade and put it back in the bag. Within seconds it filled with smoke. Stuart then made his way back over to the end of the platform and subtly dropped the bag onto the floor.

'What are you doing?' Cleo asked as he walked back over to her.

'Trust me. It's going to give us some time.'

Spotting two police officers talking nearby Stuart approached them. 'Excuse me,' he said as Cleo watched on.

'Yes sir?' replied one of the officers.

'Over there.' Stuart pointed over at where he'd just dropped the bag. By now the area around it was filling rapidly with smoke. 'I heard some men dressed in suits about taking about leaving a bomb in a bag.'

'Okay, thank you for that information sir.'

Stuart walked back over to Cleo and watched with her as the two officer approached Zachary and his suited entourage. 'That was pretty good,' Cleo admitted.

'I know.'

Not wanting to waste the time Stuart had given them, they made their way quickly across the station concourse towards

end of the line

the escalators that led down to the Underground station. Thankfully Stuart had thought ahead and bought them both travel cards on the train the night before, something he was especially glad about when he saw just how long the queue for tickets was.

Without having to wait to buy tickets, it wasn't long until they'd made their way through the ticket barriers, down another escalator and begun hearing the ode to commuting in the capital that was the 'mind the gap' announcement, as they came out onto the southbound Victoria line platform.

Although they'd just missed one train it was only a few minutes until the next one arrived, and, shortly after forcing their way onto the packed carriage, the doors closed and they accelerated into darkness.

Like everyone else on the train they remained silent as the train travelled below the city streets. It was a few stops later when Stuart tapped Cleo on the shoulder and gestured for her to follow him as the train pulled into Green Park station.

Cleo had never been to London before, and so she thought it best just to follow closely behind Stuart. While she didn't think he actually had a plan, he was at least doing a good job of pretending to know where they were going.

As they left the train, he first led her up a series of staircases before they reached a long corridor that at one end was made up a pattern of white and light blue tiles which gradually changed to white and silver at the other. After

three *by* three

walking down the corridor, they then turned right and down another short set of stairs before making a final left turn and coming out onto one of the Jubilee line platforms.

Their next train was much quieter than the first one, and neither of them had difficulty in getting a seat. Cleo spent the journey people watching as passengers got on and off at each of the stations, first Westminster, then Waterloo, Southwark. She couldn't help but wonder as she looked at each of them if any of their days were likely to be as interesting as hers.

Finally, as they left Canada Water and began making their way toward Canary Wharf, Stuart stood up and spoke for the first time since they'd left Euston. 'This is ours,' he said.

They waited by the doors until the train came to a complete stop before joining the tide of commuters making their way from the platform and up the two escalators to street level.

'Follow me. I know where we can go,' said Stuart as they walked out into daylight. 'There's a nice spot around here.'

They began walking down a nearby road until they came to a small park like area that looked out over the River Thames.

Finally feeling as though they were safe, they decided to stop for a short while to catch their breath and work out what they were going to do next.

At first, they sat on one of the benches in silence until, eventually, Stuart was the first to speak. 'I'm sorry,' he said.

'What for?' asked Cleo.

'For yesterday. I should've trusted you from the start.'

end of the line

'It's my fault that you didn't. I've given you plenty of reason not to.'

Stuart looked out at the river in front of them and noticed one of the city's commuter boats go past on it's way to Greenwich. 'I don't know why we took the train. The boat would've been much more scenic,' he said, changing the subject.

He stood up and walked over to the metal fencing that'd been put up to stop people jumping into the river. 'You know,' he said as Cleo walked over to join him. 'Yesterday I began wondering why I ever came back for you in the forest and why I ever trusted you at all. I still haven't worked out why yet, but I'm glad I did.'

'So am I.'

She smiled at him and he smiled back, then, almost instinctively, she dropped her bag on the floor and reached her arms around him to hug: and then;

Seconds later the peaceful silence was broken by the sound of guns being cocked.

They broke off the hug and looked around them.

On all other sides, they were surrounded by at least twenty men, all of them stood ready to shoot, and then, in the middle, waiting to give the order, was Zachary, also aiming a gun at them.

'I'm so sorry to break up this sentimental moment,' he said in a cold tone. He turned to one of the men who was stood

149

next to him. 'Go fetch their bag.'

Without lowering his gun, the man walked forward towards Stuart and Cleo before picking up the bag they'd dropped by their feet and taking it back to Zachary.

'That was quite a nice trick you did with the smoke,' he continued. 'But if you don't mind we'll be having the rest of our things back now.' He tipped and emptied the contents of the bag out onto the floor next to his feet. 'Well this is a shame. It does appear as though something is missing from this,' he said as he walked up to them. There was little they could do to stop as he reached into Cleo's jacket pocket and pulled out the gun she'd left in there. 'That's better. Although with your aim letting you keep it wouldn't be such a problem.'

'What are you going to do to us?' Cleo asked feeling a sudden, and surprising, sense of bravery.

'What am I going to do to you?' Zachary replied casually. 'Take a look around you. I think the question should be, what are we going to do to you... not that it should take too much effort for you to work it out yourselves.'

'Why do you want us dead?'

'My job is to neutralise threats, and that's precisely what both of you are.'

'To the country... or to you?' Cleo wasn't sure what she meant but there was a part of her that couldn't help feel as though there was another, bigger, reason why Zachary was there.

end of the line

Zachary didn't reply.

'Yesterday you told me I was free to go,' Stuart said as he too felt an unexpected burst of bravery. 'Why did you then try to kill me afterwards?'

'You were never free to go. I knew from the start that you were helping her. I just needed to find out exactly what you knew before I could do anything. Of course, it would also have been a shame to let you spoil such a nice café, so I also had to make sure it was done elsewhere.' He walked back over to stand with his men. 'Making a mess isn't such a problem here though. It's a lot easier to wash blood away from pavement compared with tartan carpet.' They watched as he raised his gun back up to aim directly at Cleo. 'Goodbye.'

Suddenly they felt as though their lives were moving in slow motion. They'd somehow managed to survive and escape what most people would've considered certain death on more than one occasion over the past few days, but this time they couldn't see a way out. They might've had the river behind them, but they knew with 20 armed men in front of them there was no way they'd be able to make it over the fence in time.

They did the only thing they could do. They closed their eyes and took a deep breath, expecting it to be their last… and then;

'Zachary,' they heard a voice say out of nowhere.

They opened their eyes. They were still surrounded.

three *by* three

'What exactly are you doing?' the voice continued.

As they looked over they noticed a woman stood behind Zachary, who himself was now wearing an irritated expression in his face.

'I'm doing my job,' he replied. 'Why are you here Marley?'

Marley walked forward towards him and signalled to the rest of the men to lower their guns, they did so immediately. 'I thought you might need some help.'

'I' perfectly fine doing this alone.'

'Yes, I can see that. It explains why you currently have twenty armed men supporting you. I'm confused though. I thought you were meant to bring them in alone, not kill them.'

'They're a clear threat,' Zachary said as he pulled out the gun he'd taken from Cleo. 'They had this in their possession.'

'And if it's now in yours then I don't see how they're still a threat.'

'How did you even find where I was?'

'I'm sure you remember all our equipment has trackers in it? I presume that's how you found them in the first place if they had that gun. I was just in my office working, saw you were close by and decided to go for a walk.'

'Can you please leave me to sort this out now?'

'Well I'm here now, I might as well help.'

a **family** reunion

Spencer Stout arrived at work early the next morning feeling a sense of both anticipation, and, to some degree, excitement too.

He couldn't help but feel as though it was going to be the day he finally found the answers he'd been working to find, it was, he thought to himself, going to be the day he finally found out who brought down that plane, and, more importantly, why as well.

Spencer was sat leaning back in his office chair and looking out over the city in deep thought when there was a knock on the door behind him.

With a small push of his foot on the floor, he swung round and noticed Marley stood at the other side of the glass with a cup of fresh coffee in her hand. He raised his hand and gestured for her to enter.

'I brought this for you,' Marley said as she handed him the coffee and took a seat opposite.

'Excellent,' he replied. 'It saves me having to go myself, thank you.' Spencer took a sip before continuing. 'Just what I need this morning, I was working quite late last night. Speaking of which I heard you were too. You should've taken the morning off to rest.'

'I was going to. I've only had a few hours sleep,' Marley replied. 'But I needed to come and speak to you.'

'Of course.' He smiled at her. 'What can I do for you.'

'It's about those two.'

'Ah,' Spencer replied. 'I presume you're referring to the two that were brought in yesterday?'

'Cleo and Stuart, yes.'

'Well, that explains why you were working so late yesterday. Have you found anything else out about them?'

'It can't be her. It just can't be. She's completely innocent, well not completely, she's done some things she shouldn't have done, but there's no way she could've brought that plane down.'

'There's no evidence she's innocent, but I must say I agree with you.'

'There's no evidence she's guilty either.'

'There's circumstance, though.'

'Not when you look into it. If it wasn't for Zachary bringing

154

a **family** reunion

her up, we'd never have suspected her.' Spencer watched as she reached into her pocket and pulled out Cleo's journal. 'And then there's this too.'

'I saw that yesterday. Where was it found?'

'In the building she was living in. We searched it on Saturday. No one was there, but we did find this.'

'She certainly spends a lot of time writing.'

'She's written about the crash. It says in this, in her words, that she didn't do it. She says she'd never have been able to do it.'

'Her words alone aren't conclusive evidence though.'

'I know. But you don't need conclusive evidence.'

Spencer thought for a moment. 'What you're suggesting isn't that simple.'

'But you know she's innocent.'

'That doesn't mean that everyone else is going to agree with me.'

'You don't need them to. It's enough if only you do.'

'What if I do and then I find out I'm wrong? What happens if she turns out not to be innocent but we only find out after it's too late to do anything?'

'You wouldn't be wrong. You know you wouldn't be wrong.'

'I'm as human as everyone. I'm not always right, I do get things wrong, and if I get this wrong, then it could be the end for all of us. Everything we do is already being watched closely by those in Government, and the public scepticism just grows each day. I have to consider everyone here. If I get this wrong, then we could all be out of a job.'

'That's a risk I'm willing to take.' She paused. 'And I know it's a risk you're willing to take too.'

'Marley,' Spencer replied in a raised voice.

'You do know who she is, don't you?... She's...' Marley fell instantly silent as Spencer raised his hand.

'Yes. I know who she is. I only found out last night though.'

'Does she know?'

'No. I don't think so. I'm planning on telling her myself later.' Spencer reached forward and drunk the rest of his coffee. 'Is there anything else you wanted to talk to me about?' he asked in an attempt to change to subject.

'Yes.'

'Is it about Zachary again?'

'Yes.'

'I don't think anyone believes he's right, but at least we can find out now.'

'He was acting strange yesterday.'

'What do you mean?'

'He didn't seem as though he wanted to bring them in. I found him ready to shoot them both.'

'Were they trying to escape?

'No. Not at that point, and he'd already made sure they weren't armed too.'

Spencer thought for a moment. 'I'll look into it,' he said. 'I

a **family** reunion

know he likes his gun, but if he's trying to kill his evidence there really might be something more going on.'

'There is something else too.'

'Yes?'

Spencer watched as Marley opened the journal to the last page Cleo had written on. 'Here,' she said showing him what Cleo words. 'She's wrote about two people she saw last Friday who she overheard talking about the crash. She doesn't say who they are, but she wrote down a description of them.'

'Do you have any ideas yourself?'

'I think he's one of them.'

'Zachary?'

'Yes.'

Spencer leant in to get a closer look and began reading for a moment before then looking up at Marley. 'Okay. I'll get this looked into as well. It may just be that he was watching the building, but if she's heard him talking then maybe not. I'll ask her about it later. It might be best not to say anything to Zachary though.'

'I understand.'

'Did you know he's been to Scotland over the weekend?'

'No. What was he doing there?'

'He was trying to find them.'

'Did he manage to?'

'Yes, he found them. Then he lost them both again.'

'What happened?'

three *by* three

'He didn't go into much detail, I think he was quite embarrassed by it, but from what I've heard they're both good at thinking on their feet.' Spencer smiled at her.

'Are you okay?'

'What do you mean?'

'Personally… After finding out about her?'

'It's given me a lot to think about. To start, I still don't know how I should tell her.'

'I can help if you want me to?'

'Thank you. I'd have already asked for your help if it wasn't for the thought that I know I'd regret not telling her myself.'

'Is there anything I can do to help?'

'Yes… there is.' Spencer took a deep breath. 'I'm going to go for a walk, I need some time to think about things this morning. Can you please make sure that when I get back though, there are two letters of closure on my desk ready to be signed.'

'You're going to do it?'

'You're right, of course you're right. I know she's innocent. If she were compared with me, she'd be the innocent one. I owe that girl a lot, and this is the least I can do for her right now.'

'I'll get them ready.'

'Marley, before you go…'

'…What is it?'

'I've heard you're spending a lot of time with one of our

colleagues recently.'

'I work with them every day.'

'I mean out of work. I wanted to ask if there's something going on there?'

'Oh… We've only met a few times. Gone out for dinner once.'

'Are you worried what others will think?'

'I… I… I just don't know.'

'There was many things your father told me while he was still alive. One of them is what he'd say to you right now if he were here.'

'What is it?'

'Love who you want and love those who hate you for it more.'

At precisely two o'clock that afternoon, Spencer was sat back in his office after a long walk, with his focus firmly on a particularly interesting article in that day's paper, that was until he heard a knock on the office door anyway.

He looked up over the top of the paper and noticed Marley stood at the other side of the glass, although, unlike that morning, she didn't have anything for him.

Spencer put his paper to one side and waved her in. 'Have you brought them with you?' he asked as he walked over to her.

'They're waiting down the corridor. Zachary is keeping an

eye on them.'

'I trust you haven't told him anything about what you said to me earlier?'

'No. Not a thing.'

'It's probably for the best. I need to speak to you about him later though. You might have been right about a few things. You haven't said anything to them either have you? Particularly her?'

'No. I thought it'd best if you say what needs saying.'

'Thank you.' He smiled at her. 'Can you bring them both in here and tell them to wait for me please, there's something I need to go sort. Oh, and can you also tell Zachary to ensure what we get some privacy too.'

'Certainly,' Marley replied.

'Much appreciated. I won't be long.'

A few minutes later, Stuart and Cleo couldn't help but feel almost surprised when they found themselves being led into the office by Marley, being treated not as suspects but as though they were guests.

'You're both welcome to take a seat,' Marley said in a tone neither of them could help but find friendly. 'Our boss will be back soon.'

'Why are you being so nice to them?' Zachary asked her under his breath.

'Because I've no reason not to be,' Marley replied. 'We need to wait outside.'

a **family** reunion

'But they can't be left.'

'Spencer asked for privacy.'

'But...'

'... Privacy!' Marley interrupted. She watched as Zachary reluctantly accepted defeat and walked out of the room to stand outside, before then turning her attention back to Stuart and Cleo. 'I'm sorry about him,' she said before also leaving the room.

Despite now being alone in the room, it was some time before either of them spoke.

'Are you okay?' Stuart eventually asked. He wasn't sure what else he could've said to break the silence.

'Yeah. Are you?' Cleo replied.

'Yeah.'

They fell silent again.

After a short time, Cleo walked over to the window and began looking at the view of London in front of her. Unsure what else to do Stuart joined her.

'That's where I work, over there,' he said as he pointed out one of the many towers making up the skyline. 'Well used to work,' he joked. 'I'm not sure I'll still have that job by the end of the week.'

Cleo looked down towards the ground. 'How far up do you think we are?'

'Fifty floors.' The answer didn't come from Stuart. They both turned to find Spencer stood by the door looking at them, two white envelopes in his hand. 'We're at the top of the building around 230 metres up,' he added as he made his way over to his desk. 'Please do both sit down.'

They remained still.

'It's much more comfortable to sit than stand,' Spencer said as he gestured towards the two empty chairs at the opposite side of his desk.

Somewhat reluctantly they both sat down.

'Why are we here?' Cleo asked almost immediately.

'You're here because I asked for you to be brought here. I want to speak to you both myself.'

'Why?'

'I've been looking at what you've both being doing over the past few days. I've also had the chance to read about your pasts...'

'... That doesn't answer her question,' Stuart forcefully interrupted. 'She asked why we're here.'

'There's sometimes I want to ask,' Spencer replied, remaining calm.

'What is it?'

'What happened? How did it get to this?' Spencer asked. 'Stuart Wright. A top city professional in your early twenties, only last week awarded a handsome bonus and earmarked for a promotion even further up the corporate ladder.'

Again, to their surprise, they couldn't help but notice, like Marley, he seemed to be speaking to them as though they were

a **family** reunion

old friends, not two suspected terrorists.'

'And then you go missing,' Spencer continued. 'You go on the run, and a few days later you end up sat in here with no reason for it...' Spencer looked down past his desk and noticed them both holding hands. 'Well, no apparent reason for it anyway.'

From his pocket, Spencer felt his phone start to vibrate. He pulled it out and briefly read the message on the screen before looking them both in the face. 'Please excuse me for a moment,' he said before pocketing his phone and making his way back over to the door.

'Excuse me,' he said to Marley and Zachary as he opened it.

'Yes sir?' Zachary replied.

'Can you please both go down to the kitchen and pick up some food for me? It's all ready and waiting.'

'Certainly sir.' Zachary turned to Marley. 'I'll be able to manage on my own,' he said before then walking off down the corridor before she'd a chance to argue.

'Well he can't cause too much harm just by fetching lunch,' Spencer said as he noticed the clear look of suspicion on Marley's face.

As he walked back into the office, Spencer couldn't help but see Stuart and Cleo were still firmly holding hands. 'Sorry about that,' he said as he sat back down. 'Where were we?'

He looked up to look Cleo in the face, as he did she did the same back. Cleo wasn't sure why but there was a part of her that felt as though she recognised him, although she couldn't think where from. Perhaps, she thought to herself, he was one of the many people she'd previously chased through the forest with an axe.

'Cleo...'

'...Yes,' she interrupted flatly.

'Grew up in care and showed promise in school. You once had hopes of becoming a doctor, but then, then it all went wrong. You ended up getting involved with the wrong people and you ended up taking the wrong path.'

'It's not always easy to take the right path when the right sort of guidance isn't there,' she replied. 'I've always had no choice but to work everything out for myself.' She watched as Spencer wiped away what she was sure was a tear from his eye. 'I never had anyone there for me. I had to give up on my dreams just so I could survive.'

Silence followed for the next few minutes until they were all relieved when Zachary broke the tension as he entered the room carrying a tray full of food and drink.

'Your food sir,' he said as he placed the tray down on the desk in front of them all.

'Thank you,' Spencer replied as he watched Zachary leave the room again, before then turning his attention back to Stuart and Cleo. 'I thought you'd both be quite hungry. You can't have had much chance to eat properly over the past few days.' He gestured towards the food. 'Please, help yourselves.'

a **family** reunion

Noticing their understandable hesitancy, he leaned forward and picked up one of the sandwiches from the tray before taking a bite from it. 'It's all okay. I've not added anything to it,' he reassured them. Stuart and Cleo remained still and continued to watch as Spencer finished off the sandwich.

Deciding it was indeed safe for them to eat, they both reached forwards for a sandwich. At the same time, Spencer made his way over to the window and began looking out at the view in thought.

After a moment he reached into his pocket and pulled out of it, Cleo's necklace, which he then began looking at. After contemplating in silence for a short time, he scrunched it up in his hand and turned back to face them both.

'I believe you used to live in an abandoned office, Cleo?'. She looked up at him but didn't say anything. 'We searched the building on Saturday and found something you left behind,' he continued as he let the necklace fall from his hand and dangle in front of her.

'That belongs to me,' she said firmly as she stood up. 'You shouldn't have it.'

'If I'm not mistake it contains a very rare stone.' Spencer began studying it closely. 'Jeremejevite, I believe. It's a stone found in only very limited quantities in the southern countries of the African continent. At a quick glance it resembles a diamond, but if you're to look closely, you'll notice something subtly different about it. It's also much rarer, and of course,

165

much more valuable than a diamond is too.'

Cleo reached out in an attempt to grab the necklace, but it was just out of reach. 'It's what my father gave me when I was left in care,' she said. 'It's the only thing I have from him. It's all I've ever had from him.'

'I'm not sure there's an easy way for me to say this, but if this necklace is indeed from your father, then I'd dare to say it's about time he returned it to you.' Spencer stepped forward s towards her and reached around her neck to attach the necklace at the back.

As he took a step back, Cleo looked down at the pendant feeling confused, and then, all of a sudden, she realised what he'd just said. 'But...' she began as she looked him in the face. She fell silent. She wasn't sure what else to say and so she looked over at Stuart, hoping he'd say something for her, but he didn't.

'Your full name is Cleo Elizabeth Stout,' Spencer continued. 'Your middle name is your mothers name. It was her idea that you should take it, it's a nice name.'

'You can't be... You're my...'

'You were born on the 31st of March, and if my memory is correct, you have a birthmark just above your left knee.'

'You're my father?' she asked before pausing and then repeating herself. 'You're my father?'

'You're my daughter.'

Despite everything that'd gone on, everything that'd been

a **family** reunion

said, and Spencer's sense of professionalism, neither of them was able to resist the impulse feeling to reach in and hug.

As he stood watching them, Stuart noticed something out of the corner of his eye: Although he was still stood outside the room, Zachary was turned to face in and was looking through the glass door at Spencer and Cleo. Stuart looked over at him, and as he caught his eye, Zachary turned back round.

It was some time before Cleo and Spencer stopped hugging, but when they finally did, overcome with emotion, Cleo walked over to the other side of the room and began looking out at the city.

Unsure if he should follow her or not, Spencer remained still for a moment before instead turning his attention to Stuart. 'Thank you,' he said as he reached out to shake his hand.

'What for?' Stuart asked.

'Protecting my daughter over the past few days.'

As he turned and walked back over the Cleo, Spencer left Stuart with a bemused look on his face. After all, Stuart was sure he'd just been thanked for protecting someone from they person they needed protecting from.

'She's out there somewhere,' Spencer said as he approached Cleo. 'Your mother I mean. She's just living an ordinary life.'

'Aren't you married to her?' Cleo asked. In her mind, she'd always expected her parents to be just like any other couple, happily married and growing old together.

three _by_ three

'No,' Spencer replied. 'We've never been married.'

'What do you mean?'

'Me and your mother, we were together for eight years before you were born. We were engaged, but we never ended up getting married.'

'Was it because of me?'

'No, not at all. It's true that we were meant to marry only a week after you were born, and we did only choose not to go through with it after you were born, but no, you're not the reason for it. The truth is, you were the reason we decided to get engaged to begin with.'

'Why have people been trying to follow us?' Cleo asked.

'I'm sorry?'

'You've brought me up here to tell me who you are, but I don't understand, why didn't you tell me earlier? Me and Stuart have been followed for days and no one ever said anything.'

'I promise you I only found out last night. If I'd have known earlier, then I'd have made sure you knew earlier too.'

'Why were we being followed at all?'

'There were suspicions that you may have been involved with bringing down a plane last year.'

'The plane my parents were on,' Stuart interrupted suddenly.

'I'm sorry to hear that,' Spencer replied. 'I'm also very sorry that I can't say I'm close to finding out who was responsible yet. It's one of the reasons I wanted to speak to you both personally though.'

'I know who brought it down,' Cleo said. 'It was the people I lived with.'

'Who are they?'

'There's Ivan, but he's the only one I know. I've seen and heard other people but I don't know who they are. I just know it was all of them working together.'

'Do you know why it was brought down?'

'I was kept out of the planning of it. I overheard them last year saying they wanted to bring a plane down, at first they spoke about forcing me to do it so that I'd take the blame for it, but then they decided I wouldn't be right, that I'd not be able to do it, even with force. It was done to be a distraction to something else they're planning though. I don't know what it is, but I heard them last week talking about making sure I'd be ready to it.'

'Do you know anything else about who they are or what they're planning? Anything at all? We're all out of leads after you.'

'No. I've tried to remember but I just can't think.'

Spencer walked over to his desk and picked up the two envelopes, one of which he then handed to Stuart and the other to Cleo. 'I know you've been through a lot the past few days being followed,' he said. 'But I hope these make up for some of it.'

three *by* three

'What are they?' Cleo asked.

'They're letters of closure. It's just a technical term really, but my job allows me to formally close any investigation into you both, permanently.'

'Do you mean a pardon?'

'Not quite. A pardon would be given when you've been found guilty of something. A letter of closure is given when you're innocent.'

'You think I'm innocent?'

'I know you're innocent. You're capable of a lot of things. That's been proven, but taking hundreds of lives? That's not something you'd be capable of.'

'How do you know?'

'Because you're my daughter.'

Cleo looked down at the envelope and then at Stuart who smiled at her. 'I still don't understand though,' she then said as she looked back at Spencer. 'If you know I'm innocent and you only wanted to ask us questions, why did you send people to kill us both?'

'Kill you both? I never sent anyone to kill you.'

'We were followed up to Scotland by your people. They tried to kill both of us. Not only then either, but again yesterday too.'

Spencer glanced across the room at Zachary stood outside. 'I knew you were followed to Scotland, but I never told anyone to kill either of you.'

a **family** reunion

'Then what was going on?'

'Right now I can't answer that. There's something I need to look into first.' He paused and then changed the subject. 'I'm sure you both must be quite tired. I've arranged for you both to be taken to a nice hotel in the city, it;s one of my favourites. There's still a lot I want to ask you both, but it's probably best if you're able to get some rest first.' He watched as Stuart and Cleo nodded at each other. 'There is something I'd quickly like to ask you though Cleo.'

'What is it?' She asked looking at him.

'When your necklace was found, we also found your journal. You'll be able to have it back of course, but for now we need to keep it for a little longer, you've written a lot of things that help us.'

'I understand.'

'Your last entry though, from Friday, I need to ask you about who you saw.'

'Oh. I really don't know who they were.'

'You did write down what they looked like though.'

'I tried to, but I didn't have a clear view at the time, I wasn't close enough.'

'I was speaking to Marley earlier this morning. She's the one stood out there,' he said pointing at the office door. 'I'm sure you'll get a chance to know her well. But she said she couldn't help but think that the description you wrote down sounded as though it could be her colleague.'

three _by_ three

'What do you mean?'

'Zachary stood out there, do you think it's possible he could've been the person you saw last Friday?'

Cleo stopped and thought for a moment as she looked over at Zachary. So much had happened over the past few days that she was able to remember very little from Friday, but as she thought about what she'd seen and heard that afternoon, she began to remember the voices of the men she'd heard talking. 'I can't,' she began. 'I can't be certain but I think I might have overheard him, I think he was one of the people I heard talking.'

'Do you mean you think he was one of the people involved in the conversation you've written down?'

'I think...'

... Cleo didn't get a chance to finish: The next few seconds happened too quick for anyone to realise what was going on.

In one swift move Zachary had opened the office door and stepped inside before firing a single gunshot at Spencer, a shot which hit him directly in the chest before continuing to smash the window behind him.

Another shot followed before Zachary fell on the floor. Marley then shot him a second time before kicking his gun across the room.

Then, as she looked up to see if Spencer was okay, she found he'd gone: The force of the bullet hitting him had been enough to knock him back and out of the window.

a **family** reunion

Both Marley and Cleo ran up to the edge and screamed as they looked down at the ground below.

'Follow me,' Marley said through adrenaline fuelled tears.

Cleo wilfully let her hand be taken and she followed Marley as she led her out of the office with Stuart behind them.

It couldn't have taken more than just a few minutes to reach the bottom of the building, but it felt, to all three of them, much, much longer.

Eventually, as the lift doors opened on the ground floor, they ran out of the building into a small courtyard outside, where they found Spencer's lifeless body lying in a pool of deep red blood and surrounded by sharp shards of glass.

Stuart stood back at first as he watched both Cleo and Marley run up towards the body and, ignoring the sharp glass around them, kneel beside it.

After a while however, not knowing what else he could do, he walked towards them and knelt beside Cleo before seconds later, she fell into a tearful heap on his shoulder.

chapter eleven
the two sisters

It had been an unusual week for Cleo. Only seven days earlier she'd been sat staring out of a cracked window in the old abandoned office block she called home, deep within one of the countries most derelict industrial estates, whereas now, 168 hours later, she was instead waking up in one of two bedrooms in a top suite within a five-star central London hotel.

She'd never felt so strange.

The week before she'd felt as though she'd nothing in life to lose but everything to gain. Now she felt as though she'd gained everything she could ever have wanted, but was already starting to lose it all again. Even Stuart had only spoken to her on a couple of brief occasions since Tuesday night.

Between them, they'd decided to spend the remainder of

the **two sisters**

the week in London. Despite now both being officially free, neither of them was able to shake off the feeling that they were still being hunted. There was also a significant number of things that Cleo could help the investigation into the plane crash with, not that she particularly felt like being much help to anyone that week.

As she sat up in her bed and looked around the room, the old antique clock on the wall chimed to announce that it was now seven o'clock. It was the day of Spencer's funeral, although it wasn't due to take place until later that day.

Although she knew she didn't need to start getting ready for some time, and despite still feeling tired, Cleo knew trying to get any more sleep would be a waste of time. She had far too much on her mind to allow her to relax enough to sleep for any longer than just a few brief hours at a time.

She'd tried many things to take her mind off of what'd happened, but all of her attempts had failed. She couldn't help but keep replaying the events of that afternoon three days earlier in her mind, and each time she did, she came up with more and more questions she wanted the answers to: Did he know it was coming? Did he feel any pain? Did he realise what was happening? And then there were other questions, questions that she couldn't help but burst into tears each and every time she thought about them: Did he miss her? Did he ever think about her? And finally: Did he love her?

Trying to concentrate on nothing but the day ahead, Cleo

three *by* three

stretched and climbed out of bed before making her way to the adjoining room where Stuart had been staying. It was empty. Wondering where he'd gone, she then walked through into their suites living area, but it too was empty.

While Stuart himself wasn't there though, she did immediately spot evidence that he had at least been there recently, because covering the entirety of the dining table in the middle of the room was a large and freshly prepared breakfast. Cleo walked up to it and as she did she noticed a small note that'd been folded and left next to one of the plates with her name scribbled on the front of it. She picked it up and began reading it;

I made this for you as I thought you'd need a good breakfast today.
I've gone for a walk, I'll be back later.

Stuart x

Cleo folded the note back up and smiled to herself as she looked down at the selection in front of her.

All the way from one side of the table to the other was plates and plates (literally) upon more plates of cold slices of meat, freshly fried bacon, thick cut toast, perfectly prepared eggs, and, in the middle of it all, a tall crystal glass jug filled with freshly squeezed orange juice that somehow Stuart had managed to remove all of the pulp from.

It looked more like breakfast for six rather than just herself,

the two sisters

although she did feel more than hungry enough to make sure that as little of it went to waste as possible. Apart from the occasional snack from the room service menu, she hadn't eaten much in days, and, if she was completely honest with herself, she hadn't eaten a filling meal in over six years.

It was nearly three hours later by the time Cleo eventually made it through the last of the muffins and showered before walking out of the hotel's front door.

She wasn't sure exactly where to go or what to do. She didn't know her way around London, and she knew she didn't have too much time to waste anyway. This was, however, the first time she'd had to herself in years, and she was determined not to first-time it.

As she set off walking through the busy streets of the capital, she couldn't help but slowly begin to realise something: In the past week she'd met her father for the first time she could remember, before then watching him die in front of her eyes, not to mention that she'd also nearly lost her own life on more than one occasion, but there she was, walking around the city as though nothing was wrong. Not one of the people she passed knew what'd happened to her, and she was almost certain none of them cared either.

She wasn't sure exactly why, but she found it reassuring.

As she looked around, she thought to herself that each and every single person that she was looking at, or at least most of them anyway, must have had, at some point in their lives, something go wrong. But then there they all were, getting on with the most important thing as though nothing had ever happened to them, they were all getting on with living. If they were able to do it, she thought, then there was absolutely no reason why she couldn't just put everything that'd happened behind her and get on with doing the same.

By the time she made it back to the hotel a few hours later, she was starting to feel much happier than she had when she woke up. Still however, as she sat down on a bench in the park square across from the hotel, her feelings quickly began to change again, and soon, with little care of who might be watching her, she let her head fall into her hands, and she began crying.

'Cleo,' she then heard a voice call out a few minutes later. At first, she presumed it was Stuart. After all, no one else knew who she was or cared enough to find out. But this couldn't be Stuart. It wasn't a man's voice.

She looked up to find Marley stood only a metre away. 'Oh… hello,' she said as she made an attempt to disguise that she'd been crying. It didn't work.

'It's okay for you to cry, we all do sometimes,' Marley said comfortingly. 'I'd be more surprised if you didn't cry on a day like this,' she continued. 'Do you mind if I join you?'

Cleo nodded.

'How are you feeling?' Marley asked as she sat down on the bench next to her.

the **two sisters**

'Different.'

'Different makes sense. Life can change quickly sometimes. Not that I need to be telling you that.'

'I just feel so strange. One minute I feel happy, as though this is everything I ever wanted, everything I've ever dreamed of having.' She stopped and thought for a moment. 'But then I also feel as though I want to go back to where I was, back to living in that industrial estate. I always wanted to know who my parents were but I never expected any of this.'

'I never had the chance to get to know my own father very well either. He died just after my fifth birthday.'

'I'm sorry.'

'Sometimes I wish he'd been there to see me grow up, and that I'd had the chance to know him properly. Then at other times I can't help but think that it would've just been much harder to say goodbye to him if I'd have fully understood what was going on.'

'My father, did he care about me?'

'Yes. He did. I promise you, he really did.'

A pregnant pause followed as Cleo thought. There was one question in particular that was on her mind, a question she wanted to know the answer to above all others. She decided to ask it straight: 'Why didn't he ever come and…'

'… See you?' Marley interrupted.

'Yes.'

'His job prevented him for a long time. It was just too

dangerous for him to risk it. Dangerous both for him, but even more so you.'

'But what about after that?'

'He wanted to. When he retired from front line work three years ago he tried to find you, but no matter where he looked he couldn't find even a single trace of you. No one could.'

'Why did he leave me in the first place?'

'Didn't he tell you that himself?'

'He said it was to keep me safe, but there must be more to it than that?'

Marley took a deep breath before continuing. 'You were born only the week after my father died,' she began.

Cleo looked across and noticed a single tear starting to run down the side of her face. 'Oh,' she said. 'You don't have to talk about it if you don't...'

'... No. It's okay. You deserve to know this.' Cleo watched as Marley wiped away the tear before she continued talking. 'When they were both younger, our fathers worked together, and they'd just returned home from a successful trip to Africa where they'd been providing security assistance to an opposition party during a country's first ever democratic election. Ultimately, the result of the election was that the opposition party won, and our fathers both had reason to celebrate. Of course, both considering themselves as traditional gentlemen, they considered a night of celebration to be a night where they shared a drink while discussing the

the two sisters

world. It was that night my father died. I was out with my mother at the time, and yours. They'd decided to go out for dinner to discuss your arrival. When we came back to my home however, we found both my father and yours lying on the floor and covered in blood. They'd been attacked by surprise. An ambulance was called, but it was too late. My father died while he was on the way to hospital, yours survived, but only just.'

'I'm so sorry,' Cleo said feeling Marley's pain.

'Your father always claimed that mine saved his life that night. Personally, I believe he'd have tried to save my father's life too.'

'What happened after that?'

'After that, your father became worried that his own family would be specifically targeted. The people who attacked them were never formally identified and so he never knew just how big the threat actually was. All he wanted to do was to keep both you and your mother safe, and so they decided to put you into care when you were born and also call of their marriage. It broke both their hearts to do it, but it was better than watching the other lose their life.'

'I don't understand though. Why didn't I just stay with my mother?'

'That's something I always wondered myself. Your father said it was because they wanted you to have the best opportunity to grow up with two parents and not just one.

three *by* three

Their hope was that you'd be adopted by a nice family while you were still young and that you'd then grow up to be their child. He'd never have openly admitted it to anyone, but I think it broke his heart again when he found out about the life you ended up living.'

'Will I be able to see her? My mother I mean.'

'Yes, I'm sure you'll be able to. We don't know where she lives at the moment though, but I'm sure we'll be able to find out for you.'

'What happened to you after your father died?'

'I can't remember much of what happened directly after, I was only young, but then neither my mother or your father could remember much either. She'd just lost her husband, and he'd just lost his best friend. I think the first few months after it happened were just a blur to everyone.'

'Did you stay living with her?'

'Yes. I know it's not going to be easy for you to hear this, but in a way, your father felt like he was mine for a time.'

'It's okay.'

'He was never a replacement of course, but he was always there for my mother and me if we needed him. My mother did actually consider putting me into care alongside you, but in the end she decided there was less risk to me because...' Marley paused. 'Because...'

'... It's okay. I understand.'

'Thanks,' Marley said as she reached into her pocket and

pulled out a tissue to wipe her eyes with. 'This isn't something I've spoken to anyone about for a long time.'

'Can I ask how you started doing what you're doing now?' Cleo asked.

'Do you mean my job?'

'Yeah.'

'That I can tell you about. Your father always kept in touch with me and my mother after my father died, he always wanted to make sure we were okay. Then one time about seven years ago, he came over to see us both. I'd just finished a degree in international relations at the time, and I was looking for a job. It just so happened that he'd been made the head of training at MI6 the week before, and so he offered me a position there and then.'

'Is that all you need to have to work for the security services?'

'I'm not exactly sure, but it might've helped that I'm fluent in six languages: Norwegian, German, French, Welsh, Spanish, and English of course... actually, it might be seven. I'm also fluent in farmyard animal.'

'Farmyard animal?'

'It's a very useful language to know. An authentic impression of a duck is just so much more effective at stopping someone from running away than a gun is. People just seem to stop and stare at me with a perplexed look on their face.'

'How did you get your current job?' Cleo asked as she tried

to stop herself from laughing.

'Well a couple of years ago the Prime Minister decided to set up a new security service that was to be entirely independent of the Government, and he asked your father to head it up. Your father then asked me to transfer from MI6 to join him.'

'What about the other person you worked with? How did he get his job?'

'Zachary?' Cleo nodded. 'Well he started about six months after I did, but he began on a much lower rank. He used to work at the UN in a counter-terrorism role before, but he decided he wanted to do much more front line work. He was good at it to begin with. That's why he was so quickly promoted. Both him and I were only just below your father, and that's not an easy job to get.'

'Why did he...'

'... I don't know,' Marley interrupted. 'Ever since it happened I've been trying to think of an answer but I can't find one.' She stopped and looked Cleo in the face. 'You saw him last week didn't you? He was the person you saw and the person you wrote about in your journal?'

'Yes. I wasn't sure at first, but I've been thinking about it ever since Tuesday, I'm sure it was him.'

'I think there's a lot more to Zachary that isn't clear yet.'

'There is still something I don't understand,' Cleo said.

'What is it?'

the **two sisters**

'Whenever he was following us, he always seemed to have other people with him and they always had guns. Why don't you have any of that too?'

'Ah… well, there's a very simple answer to that. I don't need it. I much prefer to use my head instead,' Marley joked.

'Marley, if my father acted like yours for a while, does that mean that we're sort of sisters?'

'I've never thought about it like that, but yeah, I guess we are.'

'I think you'd have made a good sister.'

'I think I probably would've too.'

Stuart arrived back at the hotel only a short while before the car that'd been arranged to pick them up and take them to the funeral.

The car was a large, jet black and sombre estate that'd been made somewhere in Germany, and had the circumstances been different, the chance to ride in such a car would've been an exciting first time experience for both of them.

'Thank you,' Cleo said as they pulled away from the hotel and onto the main road.

'What for?' Stuart asked in surprise.

'Everything you've done this week. If I hadn't met you again then I might never have had the opportunity to see my father before he died.'

'If the past week hadn't have happened, he might still be

185

alive now.'

'No,' Cleo paused. 'I think his murder had been planned for some time. What happened would've happened eventually even if we weren't there.'

They made the rest of the journey in silence, they were both in too deep a thought to attempt any more conversation.

It was only thirty minutes later when the car pulled up outside the church where the funeral was due to take place, and as they looked out of the window at the crowd gathered outside it, both Stuart and Cleo were surprised at the number of people who'd turned up.

'Are you ready for this?' Stuart asked comfortingly.

'Yes. I have to be ready.'

Cleo had never been to a funeral before, but as she walked up the path towards the church doors holding Stuart's hand, she knew that the large number of armed agents around them wasn't a presence at many of them.

'I'm sorry for your loss,' said a man dressed in a black suit as they passed him just outside the door. Although she didn't know who he was, Cleo recognised him from the group that'd been with Zachary a few days earlier, while Stuart recognised the man he'd just been talking to as the Prime Minister.

Still holding hands, they made their way into the entrance hall where they found Marley stood waiting for them along with another person neither of them had seen before.

'Cleo, Stuart, this is Holly Snow. She's my...' Marley paused for a moment. 'Friend. She works with me, and she worked with your father too Cleo.'

'It's nice to meet you Miss Stout, and you too Mr Wright. I'm very sorry for your loss,' Holly said as she reached out to shake each of their hands in turn.

By the time the service finished a few hours later it was early evening, and outside the church it was beginning to get dark. Stuart and Cleo were two of the last to file out of the building, and while much of the congregation stood around the entrance talking to each other, they instead decided to walk over to a large oak tree at the other side of the graveyard where it was much quieter.

'How are you feeling?' Stuart asked, unsure what else he could say.

'I don't know. I really don't know. How am I supposed to feel?' Cleo replied. 'How did it feel for you when you lost your parents?'

'I felt the same as you do now. I didn't ever know how to feel, not when it first happened and I still don't now. I don't think there's a way it's meant to feel.'

'Did you understand why it happened?'

'I don't think I ever will. When most people lose their parents they know it's going to happen, they expect it and they know why. All I know about my parents death it that they died in a plane crash, but I don't know why they died in that crash. I don't understand why someone wanted them and everyone

187

three *by* three

else on that plane to lost their lives.'

Stuart glanced back over at the crowd of people still stood by the church doors, as he did he noticed a woman stood on her own away from the rest of the congregation who appeared to be looking over at them both. 'Who's that over there?' he asked Cleo.

'Where?'

'That woman who's looking at us, the one who's stood way from everyone else.'

Cleo looked over at where Stuart was now pointing. She caught the woman's eye and watched as she began smiling at them. 'I don't know who she's, but she's smiling at us.'

They both continued to watch as Marley appeared from the crowd and approached the woman who, after a short conversation, soon turned their back on them as Marley began to make her way towards them.

'Marley,' Cleo said as she got close. 'Who's that woman you were speaking to?'

'Which one?' Marley asked.

'Just now.'

'Oh her, that was your father's… secretary.'

'She was smiling at us.'

'She does that. She's nice to everyone.' Marley paused for a moment before changing the subject. 'How are you feeling?'

'I still don't know how I should feel.'

'I think that's probably the way it should be.'

the **two sisters**

'What was it like when you lost your father? How did you feel?'

'I felt exactly how you do now, it's probably how Stuart felt too. You'll never be able to understand why someone chose to be responsible for taking their life. You do wonder though, you wonder so much but you can never truly understand it, even if the person who did it told you.' As she continued talking Marley reached into her jacket pocket and retrieved a small brass key from the bottom of it. 'I hope it isn't too soon for me to do this,' she said as she handed Cleo the key. 'But I'd like you to take this.'

'I don't understand,' Cleo replied. 'What is it?'

'It's the key to your fathers home, well it way anyway. It's the key to your home now. You're supposed to wait a few weeks, but I've spoken to some people, and we all agree it's okay for you to have it straight away.'

Cleo looked down at the key and then up at Marley. 'I've... I've got a home?' she asked.

'Only if you want it. You don't have to go see it straight away of course. You can go when you feel comfortable.'

chapter twelve
the mole

It had been little over twelve hours since Spencer's funeral, but already Marley was back at work early the next morning, and as she slowly dragged her feel down the corridor towards her office at the end, she knew the list of places she'd rather have been was a long one.

Despite never having felt less enthusiastic about work however, she knew there was a lot she needed to do, particularly now that Zachary was a new lead.

As she sat down at her desk, she looked at the piles of paper that were in front of her with little idea of where to begin.

'Coffee?' came a voice a few minutes later from behind her.

Marley looked round and found Holly stood by the door. 'Sorry?' she replied in a daze.

'Do you want a coffee?' Holly asked. 'I'm about to get

the mole

myself one.'

'Oh... yeah, please. The usual thanks.'

It was nearly an hour before Holly eventually returned, because while it might have been much easier and quicker for her to use the office kitchen, it was common knowledge that the best coffee came from the small café just across the road and round the corner. It wasn't so much the distance to the café that meant she might as well have bought iced coffee, but rather the time it took her to get back through all the security checkpoints.

'Thanks,' Marley said as Holly walked back into her office and handed her one of the two cups she'd bought.

'It's alright. I'm sorry it's cold though, security is slow today,' Holly replied as she took a seat next to her.

'There's a need for extra checks now, after... well, you know.'

'I still can't understand why no one's ever questioned the logic behind security checks designed to stop people carrying weapons into a place that's full of them.'

'I questioned it. It's something to do with insurance,' Marley replied as she began drinking her coffee. 'It seems quiet around here this morning. I've not seen anyone apart from you.'

'I don't think many people felt like coming in today, and everyone needs to be vetted again before coming back of course.'

three *by* three

'How did you get in then?'

'The same way that you did. Spencer trusted me.'

'He trusted Zachary too, but he was wrong about that.'

'Are you saying you don't trust me?'

'I don't know who I can trust anymore.' Marley paused then looked her in the face and smiled. 'But yes, I trust you. Of course I trust you. I just wish that Spencer had trusted me. I told him there was something else going on with Zachary. If he'd have just listened to me then maybe none of this would've happened.'

'He did trust you. You know he trusted you. You were like a daughter to him.'

'At least he had the chance to see his real daughter again.'

'How is she?'

'She's doing okay. I haven't spoken to her since yesterday. I gave her the key to his house though. I suppose it's her's now anyway.'

'What about you? Are you okay?'

'I've been better. It's not easy. If I feel like this though then I can't imagine now bad Cleo is feeling right now.' Marley paused again. 'Is it worse to lose someone you know or someone you never had the chance to know?'

Holly wasn't sure on the best way to reply, and so she settled on not replying at all. Instead, she used her sleeve to wipe away the tear that was now running down Marley's face before then changing the subject. 'What are you working on?'

the mole

she asked with interest.

'I'm still trying to find out exactly who brought that plane down.'

'Shouldn't you be looking into Zachary first?'

Marley looked her in the face. 'I am,' she said. 'I think it's the same thing.'

'You mean you think it was him?'

'Yes. I think Zachary brought it down. I think he was the only one who could've brought it down.'

'How do you know?'

'I don't for sure, but I have a hunch. I've been thinking about it for days, and it just makes sense.'

'There was obviously something else going on with him, but even with what he did to Spencer, how could it have been him? He's been working on the investigation ever since the crash, and what reason would he have?'

'He was always reluctant to be a part of the investigation at first, at times he even seemed to try stop us looking into certain possibilities as well. Then one morning he suddenly came up with the theory that Cleo was the one bending it, a young girl who's apparently capable of bringing down an entire plane on her own. I can't shake off the feeling he knew who she was long before the start of this week.'

'Didn't he spent last week following her though?'

'Yes, but that's another thing.'

'What do you mean?'

three *by* three

'He was never meant to, at least not entirely anyway. He was never meant to go up to Scotland, the only people who knew were those who went with him. And then on Monday he followed them across London, but when he found them he was about to kill them both, it was only because I turned up at the right time that he didn't.'

'He's always been someone who prefers to take direct action though.'

'But why would he be eager to shoot the person he thinks is behind it without first being able to prove it was her? They could never have escaped at that point.'

'If it was him, we're going to need proof to be able to close the investigation though, and it's only going to be harder to get now he's dead.'

'There's something else that might be some proof though,' Marley said as reached under the desk to pull Cleo's journal out of her bag. 'Last Friday Cleo wrote this,' she continued as she turned to the last entry.

Holly leant in and began reading the descriptions of the two men Cleo had seen. 'Does she think one of them was him?' she asked as she looked back up at Marley.

'I asked her about it yesterday. She said she wasn't entirely sure but now she knows who he is and she's had time to think about it, yes, she thinks one of them was Zachary.'

'There isn't another reason why he could've been there?'

'Look at what else she's written,' Marley replied as she

the mole

pointed out the previous page. 'She wrote what she overheard them talking about.'

'Most of them are too busy investigation the plane crash,' Holly read out loud. 'Is that talking about us?'

'Yes. I've read everything she's written. She said the plane crash was always meant to be a distraction away from something bigger and that they always planned to frame her for it.'

'But if it really was Zachary then that means he's be playing us along for over a year, ever since the crash happened.'

'If it's him then it means we have much bigger problems. But we need to find a way to find out for sure.'

'There's is one way to find out. All our equipment has...'

'... Trackers in it,' Marley said finishing her sentence for her. 'Can you use them to find out exactly where he's been?'

'Yes. I'll get onto it now.'

'Good. I'm going to go to Spencer's house. I always knew him as someone who always liked to work from home so there's a chance he may have found some stuff he never had a chance to share with us.'

'Number twenty-seven,' Stuart said as they pulled up on the road outside Spencer's home. 'Are you sure this is the right one?' he asked Cleo as he turned off the engine.

'Yes. That's what it says,' Cleo replied as she double checked the address Marley had written down for them the day before.

three *by* three

'Are you sure you want to do this today? His funeral was only yesterday. We can come back another day if you'd feel more comfortable.'

'I'm sure,' she replied. 'This should've been my home, and it should've been where I grew up. I've spent enough time away from here. I don't need to spend anymore.'

Although she realised the house must have changed a considerable amount since she was last there, as she climbed out of the car and walked towards it hand in hand with Stuart, Cleo couldn't help but feel a strong sense of familiarity with it. In the middle of garden, there was a large oak tree which somewhere in her distant memory she could recall seeing as a sapling when she was only a few weeks old.

They stopped for a moment outside the front door, and then, after a deep breath, Cleo reached into her pocket and pulled out the key.

'Welcome home,' Stuart said as she pushed open the door.

Cleo's first thought as she stepped inside was that the life she could've had was even further away from the one she did have that she'd first thought.

They stopped and looked around the entrance hall before making their way through the kitchen door at the other end. As she walked into the room, Cleo began to imagine how it would've felt to have walked in after a long day of school to see her father cooking their evening meal, or what coming down on Christmas morning ready to spend the day with her family

the mole

would've been like.

'Hold on,' Stuart said as he followed behind her. 'I should probably close the door.'

As Stuart left the room, Cleo remained standing still. She wasn't sure why, but she couldn't help but feel reluctant to touch anything or look at it more closely.

'Look at this,' Stuart said as he walked back into the room a minute later carrying a photo frame. 'I found it on top of the table by the door. It's the woman we saw at the funeral, the one who smiled at us.'

'Do you mean his secretary?' Cleo asked as she looked at the photo.

'Yeah,' Stuart replied as he handed the frame.

'Hold on,' she said as she noticed something written in white pen at the bottom of the photo. 'There's some names here: Spencer Stout and Elizabeth Summers.'

'Elizabeth Summers?'

Cleo paused and thought for a moment. 'Didn't we see his secretary a few days ago when we went to his office? That wasn't the same person who was at the funeral.'

'Maybe he has more than one?'

'No. I don't think she was his secretary.'

'What do you mean?'

'Look at this photo again. They're not stood as though they work with each other. This isn't his secretary. I think it's my mother. I think it was my mother who was smiling at us yesterday.'

They spent the next half hour looking around the ground floor of the house, and then, as she began looking around the first floor, Cleo found what she presumed was Spencer's bedroom.

She didn't find anything of interest as she walked in, but as she went to walk back out again, she noticed another photo frame on top of a small cabinet next to the bed. She walked up to it and picked it up. As she looked at it closely, she noticed it was a photo of her father, her mother, and most noticeably, a small baby that she could only presume was herself.

'Stuart,' she shouted out of the room.

'Yeah,' Stuart shouted back a few seconds later. 'I'm coming up.'

'You need to see this.'

'What have you found?'

'Another photo. I think this one's of me as a baby.' Cleo waited for a reply, but it didn't come. 'Stuart' she shouted out again. 'Are you coming?'

Again there was no response.

Wondering where he'd gone, with the photo frame still in hand, she walked back out onto the landing. 'Stuart, where are you?' She began walking down the stairs, but as she reached half way, she started as she heard the front door slam shut.

She could only presume he must have gone back to his car to fetch something. She made her way down the rest of the

the mole

stairs then opened the front door to look out, but while she could see his car, she couldn't see Stuart anywhere.

Cautiously she stepped outside, and then, as she made her way towards the car, she felt a hand on her shoulder.

'Well,' said a cold and unwelcoming voice. 'Isn't it nice to see you again.' Cleo turned and found herself face to face with Ivan. 'This feels almost like a family reunion,' he continued. 'You seem to be having a lot of those this week.' He paused and stared into her eyes with anger in his, then, as he noticed what she was holding, he grabbed the frame from her. 'What's this?' he asked sarcastically as he looked at it. 'Oh, it's you with your father. What a shame it will never happen again.'

Cleo reached out to take the frame back, but Ivan held it out of reach before casually throwing it back through the open door with enough force to make it smash as it hit the floor. 'You won't be needing that photo,' he joked, although Cleo didn't find it funny.

'Stuart,' Cleo shouted out in desperation.

'You can shout all you want, but your boyfriend won't be coming to help you this time. I'm afraid your family don't quite approve of him. We all feel you could do much better.'

Unsure what else she could do, Cleo turned and made a run for the main road, as she got close however, she was grabbed suddenly from both sides before she felt a light mist spray onto her face.

'Take her. I'll check the house to see if there's anyone else,'

199

three *by* three

she heard Ivan say as she fell into an unconscious sleep.

It wasn't much longer than an hour later when Marley arrived at the house.

She wasn't surprised as she walked towards the house to find the door had been left open, she presumed it just meant Stuart and Cleo were there. As she walked through the door and into the hallway however, she noticed the frame that'd been thrown on the on the floor. She bent down to pick it up, but as she did, fragments of the smashed glass fell out and back onto the floor.

'Hello,' she shouted out. 'Cleo… Stuart…' she continued shouting as she made her way into the kitchen.

Starting to feel a sense of worry at the lack of response, she walked back into the hallway and then up the stairs to the first floor. 'Is anyone here?' she called out as she reached the top step, but again, she didn't receive any reply.

Feeling more concern as each second passed, she walked up another set of stairs to the top floor where she knew Spencer's study was.

His study was a large room, but one that could also be described as cosy. It was full of antique furniture and bookcases filled with titles on nearly every subject imaginable. The only thing in the room that wasn't old or traditional was the laptop he kept on the top of his desk by the window, and it was this that Marley was interested in.

the mole

She was pleased with herself at being able to remember his password on her first attempt, but as she opened up the footage for the CCTV she knew he'd installed, she only felt panic.

She rewound the footage back and began watching as it showed a large white van with an obscured number plate pull up on the road, out of which climbed three men who then disappeared from view as they walked towards the house. They were only out of sight for a short time however because before long they appeared from the house, dragging Stuart behind them towards the van. Marley continued to watch as a few minutes later, Cleo also emerged from the house, and despite putting up a flight, was also dragged into the van.

Knowing she needed to do something quickly, Marley closed the laptop and made her way back down to the kitchen.

As she walked into the room, she pulled her phone out of her jacket pocket and quickly dialled Holly's number. 'Holly, they've been taken,' she said as the call connected. 'I don't know who by, but it was in the last couple of hours. Cleo should still have the key I gave her. It's got a tracker in it, can you find where they've been taken?' Suddenly out of the corner of her eye, she noticed something that'd been left on the kitchen table. 'Actually,' she continued. 'She doesn't have it. The key's here.'

chapter thirteen
the end

Marley felt angry when she arrived back at her office. She was angry with herself. She was meant to be making sure they were safe, meant to be making sure they were protected, and she'd failed. Not only did she feel as though she'd let down both Cleo and Stuart, but she also felt as though she'd let Spencer down too. She'd let herself become so distracted by what was on her mind that she'd completely forgotten about what she should've been doing, and now she'd no idea where they were and only a little idea of who'd taken them.

Holly was still busy working on her computer as she walked into the room. 'We need to find them, and we need to do it straight away,' she said as she sat down next to her. 'If this is all a part of something bigger then we need to work quicker than we've ever worked before,' Marley continued.

the end

'I think I've got a way we can trace where they are,' Holly replied.

'How? They don't have anything on them that they can be traced by. The only thing they had was the key, and that was left in the house.'

'There's a chance one of them may carrying something internally that we can trace though.'

'Internally? What do you mean internally?'

'I've been looking through our CCTV, there's something quite interesting from the other day,' Holly replied as she opened up a new screen on the computer in front of them.

As Marley leant in closer to look at the screen, Holly clicked to begin playing the footage. Marley looked closer still and noticed that it showed Zachary preparing what appeared to be a tray of food. 'I don't understand,' she said looking up at Holly.

'Take a closer look,' Holly replied as she reached in and pressed the screen to make it zoom on Zachary's hand. 'Just... there. Into one of the drinks, he adds something.'

'When's this footage from?'

'Tuesday afternoon at around quarter past two.'

'That was when Spencer was talking to Cleo. He asked Zachary and me to go pick up some food from the kitchen for them. Zachary insisted he could do it alone though.'

'Well now you know why.'

'But what did he add? Was it a poison of some sort?'

three *by* three

'It can't be a poison. None was found in Spencer's body and if it'd been Cleo or Stuart who'd taken it they'd have been dead within an hour.' Marley watched as Holly reached into her pocket and pulled out a small case around half the size of her hand. 'I think it was one of these. I found them in Zachary's desk.'

Marley reached in and took the case from her. As she opened it she found herself looking at a number of tiny metallic devices no bigger than a single hundred and thousand. 'But these are microphones,' she said as she looked back up at her. 'They're mini microphones.'

'He was listening in to everything that was being said in that room. He knew exactly what they were talking about.'

'Are the recordings saved anywhere?'

'Yes. I've already listened to it.'

'What were they talking about?'

'Spencer began by telling Cleo who he was and then they began to speak about family.'

'That won't have been of any interest to Zachary.'

'Then they started talking about the plane. He'd just given them both their letters of closure. Then he asked her about the crash and what she knew about it. Cleo said she didn't know who'd brought it down but that she'd seen people and heard things.'

'That's what she told me yesterday too.'

'Spencer then brought up something you'd mentioned to

204

the end

him, about one of the people Cleo saw being Zachary.'

'I showed him what she'd written in her journal. It was what I showed you earlier.'

'He asked if she thought it could be him.'

'And what did she say?'

'She said she couldn't be sure, but it could've been.'

'Yesterday she said the more she thought about it, the surer she felt it definitely was him.'

'Spencer also asked her if he'd been the one she'd overheard talking, but she never got a chance to answer, that was when Zachary made his move.'

'Do you mean Zachary killed Spencer to protect himself?'

'It seems that way. Spencer was already suspicious about him. You weren't the only one who said there might have been something going on. If Cleo said it as well, then he'd have known for sure.'

'But this is Zachary. He must have known that I'd have done what I did after, and he's never seemed the sort of person who'd give up his on life so easily, not when there was still so little real evidence against him anyway.

'I think that's what we should be worried about. If he was willing to give up his life what was he giving it up for? He's been trying to distract us from something for months and months, and right now we're in a position where whatever it is might be about to happen but we've no idea what it is, we can't question him, and we're down to just two people.

three *by* three

'He hasn't been trying to distract us. He has been distracting us.'

'How do we find out what from?'

Marley looked back down at the microphones. 'How long do these stay in the body for?' she asked.

'It should be around seven days.'

'Can you trace the one Zachary used?'

'Yes, but only if it wasn't Spencer who ingested it.'

'Okay, get on to it. I'm going to have a look around Zachary's office to see if there's anything else that'll help us.'

Cleo couldn't have been sure exactly how long she'd been unconscious for when the eventually came round, but she did know, at the very least, it was longer than just a few minutes.

She was lying face down on a cold stone floor in a pitch dark room, although she wasn't able to make out any of the walls to see how big the room was.

She made an attempt to sit up, but it was impossible. Both her arms had been tied together behind her back.

'You won't be able to untie the rope,' she heard a man's voice say out of nowhere from the other side of the room. 'I've been trying to untie mine for days.'

'Stuart?' Cleo replied hopefully, although she was almost certain it wasn't him.

'No. I'm not Stuart. My name is James,' the man replied. 'I presume Stuart is the other person you were brought here

the end

with. He was taken not long ago.'

'Taken?' Cleo replied sounding worried. 'What do you mean taken? Taken where?'

'I can only think that they want to ask him some questions. They'll bring him back soon enough, but I can't guarantee he'll be in the same condition he was when he left though.'

'What's going on? Where are we?'

'I can't answer either of those questions. I've spent days wondering myself. I can tell you who brought you here though.'

'I already know who brought me here. It was my family.'

'Your family?' James asked in surprise.

'Well not my real family. I lived with them though, and they always called themselves my family.'

'Ah… you must be Cleo then?'

'How do you know my name?'

'I've heard my brother talking about you.'

'Your brother?'

'Yes. He's the one who brought me here.'

'You mean, you're Ivan's brother?'

'Oh, Ivan no. My brother is Issac.'

'I was brought here by Ivan.'

'I know him. Ivan and my brother have been friends with each other for as long as I can remember, ever since they started school. Ivan did always seem strange.'

It was just over half an hour later when Marley walked back

into her office holding a piece of paper she'd found in Zachary's office, and while she still felt angry with herself, by now, she also felt determined to put it right.

'Did you find anything?' Holly asked as she watched Marley sit back down next to her.

'Yes, but it's not good,' Marley replied as she handed her the paper. 'I think this proves it was Zachary who brought the plane down and how he did it too.'

Holly looked down and surveyed what she'd been handed before looking back up at Marley with a much more concerned look than before. 'But this,' she began. 'This is an authority to bypass airport security.'

Marley nodded. 'It's from the day of the crash.'

'What time did the plane leave?'

'It should've left at 14:25, but it was delayed by 17 minutes and left at 14:42.'

'And this is from?'

'Just over three hours before it left.'

'He could've taken anything though.'

'Whatever he took through was what brought that plane down.'

'But why was this never found as part of the first investigation? Surely the airport must have thought this was something important?'

'They thought we already had it.'

Holly paused for a moment. 'Because he requested it?' she

the end

asked.

'Yes, and he's been keeping it out of sight ever since.'

'But what about the wreckage? If he placed something onto the plane to bring it down then we'd have found it among the debris at the crash site.'

'Not necessarily. He kept going back to the site alone. He had the chance to make sure anything there was hidden too.'

'All of this, but why? What's he been distracting us from? We still have no idea.'

'Are you any closer to finding where they?'

'Yes. I don't know which of them ingested the microphone, but I've got a signal from it. It's just loading down.' Holly reached over and picked up a small tablet device from the other side of the desk. 'And it's just done,' she continued. Marley watched as she pressed on the screen, as she did a map appeared with a dot in the middle of it indicating the location of the signal.

'It looks as though they're in a warehouse,' Marley said as she looked in closer.

'It's to the east of us, about thirty miles.'

'If it's a microphone are we able to listen in?'

'We should be able too... hold on...' Holly pressed on the screen again, before a few seconds later they could start to hear Cleo's voice crackling through the speakers.

'When did they take him?' they heard Cleo say, although they weren't sure who she was asking.

three *by* three

'Just over an hour ago,' a man's voice responded. 'It wasn't too long before you woke up.'

'How long have you been here?'

'Three days. My brother turned up at my house on Wednesday night. I can't remember much of what happened though. I opened my front door, and then I woke up here.'

'Who's your brother?'

'Issac. Issac Urwin.'

Without delay, as she heard the name Holly began typing it into the computer on Marley's desk in front of her. 'Got it,' she said shortly afterwards. 'Issac Urwin, his father was Simon Urwin, the entrepreneur. He's got one brother called James, an inventor, he must be the other person we can hear.'

'Can you find out if there are any connections to Zachary?' Marley asked.

'I'll do it now,' Holly replied as she began typing again.

Suddenly Marley and Holly turned all their attention back to the tablet as a loud bang came from the speakers. 'I think they're bringing him back,' they then heard James say afterwards.

'Stuart,' Cleo said. 'Are you okay?'

'I'm fine, I think,' they heard Stuart reply. 'Have they done anything to you?'

'No.'

'Good. I'd rather they did it to me.' Marley and Holly leant in closer to the table and waited as Stuart paused. 'I... I know

the end

you,' he eventually continued. 'You're James Urwin. I saw you in the paper the other day.'

'You know who he is?' Cleo asked.

'Yes, he was in the paper on Monday morning. I can't remember exactly what it was but he invented something, I think it was a battery powered by hydrogen or something like that.'

'I didn't invent it alone. My brother helped,' James replied.

'Your brother?'

There was a cough as someone cleared their throat before another voice began speaking. 'Well as we seem to be introducing ourselves right now. Hello, Cleo, I believe it is? I'm Issac. We've not had the chance to formally meet before now, but…'

'… I've seen you,' Cleo interrupted. 'I saw you last week. You were with someone else.'

'I was just about to say that,' Issac replied in a cold voice. 'You saw me with the late Zachary Jones. It's a shame about his death. He was good at what he did, but at least he managed to take someone else with him.' Issac laughed to himself. He knew he'd just hit a nerve with at least two of the people in the room and there was nothing either of them could do about it.

'Issac, what's going on?' James asked. 'It's bad enough you've brought me here, but bringing these two as well?'

'They were becoming an inconvenience for me, James.'

'Why did you kill my parents?' Stuart asked suddenly.

211

three *by* three

'Oh...' Issac replied in surprise. 'I killed your parents? I didn't know I had. When was this?'

'That plane. You were the one who brought that plane down. My parents were on it.'

'I'm afraid you're wrong about that. I didn't bring it down. It was done by Zachary.'

'Zachary?' Cleo and Stuart said together.

'Wasn't it obvious? He was the only one who could bring it down. His job allowed him certain privileges. Privileges that ensured he was able to put everything in place that needed to be in place and hide any evidence of course.'

'Why that plane though?' Stuart continued. 'Why did you target that plane?'

'I overheard you,' Cleo began. 'I overheard you talking about it being a distraction away from something else.'

'It was more than just a simple distraction. A distraction could've been easily achieved by bringing any plane down. That plane was chosen specifically.'

'What was so special about it?' Stuart pressed.

'The passengers.'

'My parents?'

'No, not your parents. They just happened to be in the wrong place at the wrong time. Collateral damage I think it'd be called...'

'... How can a life be considered collateral damage?'

'Be patient, I'll show you later on,' Issac paused. 'On that

the end

particular plane there were two people I did want to target though,' he continued.

'Addison and Koller.' This time it was James that spoke up.

'Oh… very good James,' Issac replied. 'I'm surprised you know that.'

'Hugh Addison and Miles Koller. I saw their names in the paper the day after the crash.'

'I don't understand,' Stuart said. 'What's so important about them? Why would they be targeted?'

'They were my father's business partners, his advisers, his friends… Issac why would you want to kill them?'

'That's an easy question to answer. They both deserved to die, and they both deserved to suffer, and so did their families.'

'What are you talking about?'

'Surely you haven't forgotten how our father died James?'

'He took his own life.'

'Because he felt as though he'd no other choice.'

'I still don't understand?'

'His business and his life collapsed. That was what made him feel as though he'd no option. But it wasn't his fault. It was the fault of the people he worked with too.'

'That's why you killed them? That isn't a reason to take anyone's life.'

'It's more than a reason. When our father's life collapsed, they were able to keep living as though nothing had ever gone wrong. Why should our father have been the one forced to take his own life when the people who forced him were able to keep theirs?'

'They didn't force him to do anything. No one forced him to do anything.'

'This still doesn't make any sense,' Stuart interrupted. 'What about me? What about Cleo? What have we done?'

'You,' Issac replied. 'You got in the way. Your friend was meant to be my goat in all of this. While Zachary's position allowed him to ensure the plane came down, it also allowed him to make sure that all the evidence was planted firmly on one person.'

'Why me though? Cleo asked. 'Why did you choose me?'

'Because you were easy to choose. A simple minded girl. Of course, it wasn't entirely random. I knew I needed help with what I had planned and so I came to Ivan, an old school friend of mine. I knew he'd got involved with crime and so it didn't take too much convincing, or too much money, to get him on board. You were just someone he was happy to try and get rid of.'

'This isn't just about that plane though,' Cleo replied. 'I've overheard more. The plane was just meant to be a distraction. Ivan was trying to get me ready for something else, whatever the plane was a distraction from.'

'You know more than I thought. Maybe you aren't quite so simple minded after all.'

'What was it? What was he trying to get me ready for?'

the end

'He was getting you ready for something that'll still happen whether you're ready or not...'

'... Issac, you can't kill anyone else,' James interrupted.

'I'm going to take the life of every singe person who deserves to have it taken from them. Every last person who has our father's blood on their hands will be dead by the end of today.'

'No one is responsible for what happened.'

'But they are. His business partners, they directly advised him, it was their advice that led him to where he ended up.'

'But what happened was a recession. It wasn't caused by them...'

'... Exactly. They weren't entirely responsible. Only partly. The rest of the blame lies with those who caused that recession.'

'No one person cause it.'

'Which is why I'm not going to waste any time trying to narrow it down at all.'

'What do you mean?'

'Today I'm going to make sure that each and every single person who caused our father to take his last breath will take their own, and I don't care how many others do if they get in the way.'

'You can't do that. By that thinking you'd have to kill everyone in London...' A pregnant pause followed as James realised. 'Issac... you can't be thinking that.'

three *by* three

'I'm thinking exactly that.'

'You can't do that. There are millions of innocent people. Everyone is innocent. No one caused our fathers death and no one deserves to die.'

'How could you even do that?' Cleo asked. 'It's impossible.'

'Impossible? No,' Issac replied. 'That's where my brother comes in, and you of course.'

'I am never going to help you with something like this,' James said.

'But you already have.'

'What do you mean?'

'Your inventing. You invented a device that stores a significant amount of compressed gas, gas which, it just so happens, is highly flammable and explosive, and thanks to a small feature I've added...'

'... What feature?'

'A feature which allows me to release that gas remotely from every single device at the same time.'

'But those devices are all over the city. There's thousands of them. If they all empty at the same time, the entire city could go up in one bang.'

'Exactly! Quick and efficient.'

'But where do I come into this?' Cleo asked.

'You were meant to be the one who actually released it all. Unfortunately, the remote signal only has a limited range.'

'You'd have to force me to.'

the end

'That's exactly what I was planning on doing. As it happens, I don't need you anymore though. There's another way I can do it myself without too much risk to my own health.'

'What way?'

There was another sudden bang before a fifth voice began to speak. 'Issac. It's ready to go.'

'Ah. Excellent,' Issac replied to the voice. 'Thank you Ivan.'

As the conversation fell silent, Marley and Holly leant back and looked each other in the face.

'I've found it,' Holly said gesturing towards the other screen. 'Issac and Zachary knew each other. They lived together while at University.'

'We need to find them and stop this.'

'We can't, not that easily. There's only you and me right now. We'll never be able to do it alone.'

Marley stopped and thought for a moment. 'Usually I'd think we'd be all that's needed, but you're right, this is bigger. I'll get on the phone to MI5.' She said as she stood up to leave the room.

'Hold on,' Holly called after her as there was a beep from the tablet. 'They're moving.'

'Moving? What do you mean moving?'

'They're gaining altitude and speed.'

'Where are they moving towards?'

'It looks as though they're heading for London. According to this, they'll come straight over the top of us.'

three *by* three

'How far away are they?

'Currently 20 miles, but they're moving quickly. They can't be more than a few minute away.'

'We need to get to the roof.'

Making sure to bring the tablet, Holly stood up and followed her out of the room and up a nearby set of stairs until they came to a door at the top of the building.

'They're about 30 seconds away,' Holly said looking down at the screen as they walked out into the breeze at the top of the building. '25… 20…'

Before there was a chance for either of them to say anything else, there was a loud rumbling from above as a large green military style transportation helicopter flew past overhead.

'Is that them?' Marley asked in disbelief as the watched it fly off towards the city.

'This says it is.'

'Okay, follow me,' Marley said as she grabbed her arm and led her around the corner to the helicopter pad that was at the other side of the roof. 'Are you any good at flying?' she continued.

'Flying? Flying what?'

'Helicopters,' Marley replied as she gestured towards the jet black chopper that was on the pad in front of them.

'Me? But I'm not a pilot. I've never flown anything before. I'm just a junior agent.'

the end

'Congratulations on the new promotion then,' Marley said as she reached in to shake Holly's hand. 'Climb in.'

Holly wasn't given a chance to argue. Marley had already walked off to climb into the back of the helicopter, and so, somewhat reluctantly, she made her way to the front and climbed into the cockpit.

'I've no idea what I'm doing here Marley,' she said as she surveyed the controls and dials in front of her with little idea of what any of them did or were telling her.

'Don't worry. I'll guide you through it.'

'What are you doing?' Holly asked as she looked back into the cabin behind her.

'I'm making sure this is fully loaded,' Marley replied as she grabbed what appeared to be a sniper from a shelf on the cabin wall.

By the time Marley and Holly had finally got into the air, the helicopter they were meant to be following had already made it's way to the centre of the city.

'I really should thank you, James. Those helicopter lessons you bought me for my birthday are coming in useful,' Issac said as he stuck the helicopter onto autopilot and made his way back into the cabin. 'It certainly makes everything easier anyway. One less person is needed, one less person who could make it all go wrong.'

'I still don't understand why you're doing this,' James said as he looked his brother in the face. He, Stuart and Cleo were all sat on the cabin floor with their arms tied behind their back while Ivan stood a short distance away keeping a gun aimed at them.

'I've already told you,' Issac replied. 'It's about time that somebody else suffered for once.'

'I suffered. I'm suffering now. Isn't that enough for you?'

'I want to see more than just you suffer James. I want to see every singe person who's below us suffer.'

'But they haven't done anything wrong.'

'They made me suffer, and they made our father suffer, they even made you suffer. How can you not see that?'

'I still don't understand what you mean.'

'Then let me explain it to you one final time. Eighteen years ago our father died. Everyone told us it was suicide. They always told us it was suicide, but it wasn't, I know it wasn't and you know it wasn't too. It was murder. Our father was murdered. He was murdered by those who right now are walking below us, by those who carried on as though nothing was ever wrong while in reality, they were making this country collapse. They made our father's work collapse, and they made his life collapse too, and then, to finish off, they drove him to the end.'

'What happened was no one's fault Issac, you need to realise…'

'… How can you say that?' Issac interrupted. 'How can you sit and say that it was no one's fault. These people, these

the end

murderers, they took your father from you.'

'Do you think this is what he'd have wanted? What he'd have wanted his son to do?'

'I never got the chance to know what he'd have wanted. That chance was taken from me like it was taken from you.'

'Issac, I trusted you.'

'You believed me.'

'I thought you wanted to help make the world a better place. I thought you wanted to put his money to good use and help create a legacy that out family name could be proud of.'

'A legacy? You call it a legacy? You used his money to invest in those who caused his death. You used his money to improve the lives of those who ruined ours and ended his. That isn't a legacy. That's an insult. I used his money to make sure those who made us suffer and those who made him suffer will suffer themselves. That's a true legacy. A reminder that they can't all just keep living each day as though they never did anything wrong, as though what they did will never have any consequences. It started with his business partners, and today, it's going to end with the population of London.'

'But there are millions of innocent people in London.'

'Innocent? We were the innocent ones. What did we ever do to deserve what happened to us?'

'We didn't do anything, but neither did anyone else. Nobody ever wanted our father to die. No one ever wanted that to happen.'

three *by* three

'He did. He wanted it to happen. He wanted his life to end. That's why he ended it. But he didn't do it for no reason. He wanted to end it because he was pushed to end it.'

'Is this what you want your legacy to be? Do you want to be remembered as the person who killed millions of innocent people?'

'Today isn't going to be my legacy… it's going to be your's James. I have absolutely no intention of today being my last, but I do have every intention of making sure it is for you, and just like our father didn't, I'm going to make sure you don't get a chance to defend yourself either.'

'I don't need to defend myself. I've done nothing wrong.'

'But don't you see? You're going to be the one who's at fault. You were the one who designed those devices. You were the one who designed them to be able to release the hydrogen.'

'You helped to create them. The release was your idea.'

'I wasn't helping you. You were helping me without even realising it. You decided to listen to me over all of the experts, every single one of them said adding a way to release the *highly flammable gas* from its *protective chamber* was a stupid and dangerous thing to do, but you ignored them and listened to me. That's what your legacy will be, allowing a device that can destroy a city to be created. Only, of course, people won't ever know it was never your idea in the first place.'

'Issac, you can't do this.'

'I can do whatever I want and right now what I want to do

the end

is watch as millions of people suffer like we did, as they lose their lives, as their families lose their lives, and then, after we've all watched together, you're going to join them.'

'Why are you doing this to me?'

'Because you helped these people. You socialised with these murderers. You're no better than them, and today, you're going to die with them.'

They all watched as Issac reached into his pocket and pulled out a small device with a single button on it. 'All it's going to take is one push on this and every device will instantly release what it's storing. After that, all it'll take is a single spark to set it off, it could be a match, an overhead wire, even a phone signal would be enough.'

Issac made his way over to one of the cabin windows and looked out at the city below. 'Oh,' he said looking back at Stuart and Cleo on the floor. 'Please don't be thinking either of you will be surviving the day.' He laughed to himself and looked back out as he pressed the button. At first, he was surprised when nothing happened, and then, as he tried pressing it a second time, his surprise quickly turned to anger. 'Ivan, why hasn't it worked?' he forced through gritted teeth. 'Nothing has happened. WHY?'

'I... I have no idea,' Ivan replied sounding a mix of both confused and, more noticeably, scared. 'It should've worked. The devices are all over the city. There's thousands of them.'

Issac looked down in turn at Stuart and Cleo, then, as he

223

three *by* three

looked his brother in the face, he noticed a subtle smile. With anger, he stood forward and dragged James to his feet before pushing him up against the cabin wall. 'Why are you smiling?' Issac asked slowly.

'Because you can't make it work, not from here.'

'What do you mean? Why won't it work from here?'

'It never will.'

'Why not? What are you talking about?'

'It looks as though you never designed it to work from so high up. The signal isn't strong enough at this height, and it never will be.'

James fell back to the floor as Issac released his grip. 'Well we're just going to have to go lower then,' he said as he made his way back towards the cockpit.

'You can't,' James called after him. 'You'd be committing suicide if you did that.'

Issac stopped with his hand on the cockpit door. 'How high would it reach?'

'At least double how low you'd need to go.'

Issac paused and took a deep breath before turning back to face his brother. 'Well then,' he said walking back towards his. 'If we can't all go that low then I'll just have to make sure one of us does.' He reached forward and pulled James back to his feet before dragging him towards the exterior door.

'No one's going to be able to get low enough unless they jumped out.'

the end

'That's exactly what I was thinking,' Issac replied as he grabbed the handle of the door and slid it open. As he did, there was immediately a rush of cool air into the cabin and the entire helicopter began to shake.

'You're not expecting me to jump are you?' James said as he looked out. 'We're hundreds of metres up.'

'Only nine hundred. You'll have long enough to press the button before you hit the ground, and if you fail, well at least I'll have another two tries,' Issac replied as he glanced back at Stuart and Cleo.

'Have you gone insane Issac? Why would I do it?'

Issac took a step forward and reached to untie the ropes holding James's hands behind his back. 'You're going to end up dead by the end of today no matter what,' he then whispered into his ear. 'Personally, I'd rather you took a few more people with you at the same time.'

'Personally, I'd rather die alone.'

'Then that can be easily arranged for you.'

James watched as Issac reached into his jacket pocket and pulled out a loaded gun before pointing it at his chest.

'If you kill him this won't work Issac,' Ivan suddenly interrupted. 'He needs to be alive to press the button.'

In rage Issac suddenly turned and aimed at Ivan. 'DO NOT TELL ME WHAT I SHOULD BE DOING!' he screamed at him. 'I will kill whoever I want to kill today, and I make no guarantee that you're excluded from that.' He took a deep

225

breath then turned back to face his brother, but as he did, he found James had gone.

He stepped forwards and, looking out over the edge towards the ground below, he noticed James falling through the air before suddenly, he disappeared from view as a parachute opened above him.

Glancing up, Issac noticed a number of parachutes hanging from the cabin wall next to the door. 'He's taken one of them,' he said as he stared at Ivan. 'WHY ARE THERE PARACHUTES HERE?'

In anger, he leant back out the door and shot towards his James in a blind rage, but knowing he had little chance of hitting his brother from that distance, he reloaded his gun and then turned his attention to Cleo. 'Stand up,' he spat at her. 'It was always meant to be you who did this from the start so you might as well be the one to have a go next. Ivan, untie her hands,' he said as he made sure not to take his focus, or aim, off her.

'I'm not doing anything for you,' Cleo replied defiantly as Ivan forcefully pulled her to her feet. 'You can throw me out, but I'll be throwing that device away.'

'Then I'll throw you out now and give the job to your friend after you've died,' Issac said as he used his free hand to pull her towards the open door.

'I'm not doing anything for you either,' Stuart said as Ivan swung round to hit him.

the end

'You're going to kill both of us no matter what we do now,' Cleo continued.

'That's true. But if you refuse to do this for me.' Isaac began whispering into her ear as he moved his gun up to aim at her temple. 'Then I'll make sure both your death, and his, are as slow and painful as I can make them.'

'If that saves everyone else's life then you can make taking mine as painful as you want.'

'You're mistaken if you think it will save anyone's...'

Suddenly Issac was interrupted by the sound of a gunshot.

Cleo looked down expecting to see blood dripping from somewhere on her body, but she couldn't and she didn't feel any pain either. She hadn't been the one who was hit. She looked back up at Issac, and as she did, she noticed a large wound on the side of the arm he was holding his gun with.

'WHERE DID THAT COME FROM?' Issac shouted out in pain.

'I... I don't know,' Ivan replied.

All three of them looked out of the door and noticed for the first time, flying close by, another helicopter, this one being piloted by Holly. Then, as he looked towards the back of it, Issac also noticed Marley laying down and aiming straight at him.

Using the remaining strength in his other arm Issac raised his gun again, ready to shoot at anything in rage, but, before he had the chance, he felt a single sharp and hard blow to his

three *by* three

face as Cleo swung round and hit him as hard as she could.

Caught off guard Issac lost his balance and fell to the floor. Seconds later however, he'd pulled himself back up and, using all his strength, he held his gun up to Cleo one final time before Marley pulled the trigger again, this time however, she hit him in the middle of the stomach. He looked down to see his shirt quickly turning red, and then, unable to stop himself, he fell forward, past Cleo, and straight out of the open door.

Briefly, Cleo leant out of the door and looked down to see Issac falling away from them at an ever-growing speed. But then, just as she began thinking she and Stuart were now safe, she remembered that Ivan was still with them.

Although he was still armed with his own gun, as she looked at him, Cleo couldn't help but think that he seemed to have lost much of his usual confidence.

She watched as slowly, and somewhat shakily, Ivan raised his gun and aimed it at her. 'Give me one of those parachutes,' he said gesturing towards the two remaining ones on the wall.

'You can't run from this. You're as much responsible as he was,' Cleo replied. 'You ruined my life, and you helped to try ruin millions more. I'm not letting you run away from this.'

In a panic, Ivan suddenly put his arm down and aimed at Stuart instead. 'If you don't give me one of those parachutes, you're going to watch him die in front of you.'

'I can't let you run. You've done too much to run.'

'I can still do much more if you don't.'

the end

Cleo remained defiant. And then, as Ivan began staring into her eyes with rage in his, he suddenly tripped and fell forward as Stuart swung round on the floor and knocked his legs, and although he didn't hit the floor very hard, it was enough to make him lose his grip on his gun as it slipped forwards out of his hand and, more importantly, out of this reach.

Taking her chance while Ivan was busy pulling himself back up, Cleo stepped forwards and kicked the gun sideways out of the door, but as she went to look back at him, she then felt herself being grabbed by the throat and thrown across the cabin with force.

For a short moment her vision went blank, and then as it came back, she realised there was little more she could do than watch as unimpeded Ivan grabbed one of the parachutes before then, after taking the chance to kick Stuart in the side, he disappeared from view as he jumped out of the door.

'Stuart,' she called out after catching her breath. 'Are you okay?'

'Yeah. He just kicked me, but I'll be fine,' Stuart replied in clear pain. 'Are you okay?'

'My head's bleeding I think, but I'll be fine.'

'Can you untie me please?'

Ignoring her injuries, Cleo pulled herself to her feet and slowly made her way over to Stuart.

'Thanks,' he said as she first untied the ropes binding his

legs and then the ones holding his arms behind his back. 'I'm sorry I couldn't be of more help.'

'You were as much help as you could be,' she said as she helped him to his feet.

'What do we do now?' he asked as he straightened himself up. 'We can't stay stay up here forever.'

'I don't know. But I need to check something.'

'Okay,' Stuart replied in confusion. 'I'll see if I can find any more parachutes.' He watched as Cleo then walked over to cockpit before turning his attention to a cupboard at the other side of the cabin.'

'Stuart, this probably isn't going to stay in the air for much longer,' Cleo called back from the cockpit a few minutes later. 'There isn't much fuel left.'

'Then we need to get out before it runs out completely,' Stuart replied as he continued searching the rest of the cabin for more parachutes. He looked up as Cleo walked back from the cockpit with a grave look of worry on her face. 'I can only find one more,' he continued. 'We're going to have to share it.'

'No,' Cleo replied. 'You need to use it.'

'It's okay. We can share it.'

'Stuart listen to me,' she began as she looked into his eyes. Stuart had gotten to know many of her facial expressions well over the past few days, but at that moment he found himself looking at one he'd not seen before, and one he didn't understand. 'You need to jump... alone.'

the end

'But what about you?' he replied. 'You can't stay in here when it falls. You'll be killed.'

'Probably. But if it just falls out of the sky then so would anyone who's below us. We're above one of the world's most crowded cities, if it falls out of the sky here, it's going to kill more than just a few people.'

'But what are you going to do? You can't fly a helicopter.'

'No I can't, but I can at least try to do something, and that's better than doing nothing at all.'

'Cleo you can't try. You mustn't try, please, don't try.'

'Listen to be,' she said as a tear began to run down her face. 'When all of this is over I'm still not going to have a family, I'm still not going to have anywhere to go...'

'... But...'

'...NO! For you too long I've been causing people pain. I've been involved with all of this from the start, and that makes me responsible for it, even if it wasn't by choice.' Cleo looked him in the eye and noticed for the first time since she'd met him, he too also had a tear running down his face. 'I may not have been able to do anything before, but this time I can. This time, just this time, I'm going to be the one who saves lives. I'm sorry, but you need to trust me. I need to do this.'

She looked him in the face one final time and then, without saying anything else, she turned and to walked back towards the cockpit. As she reached for the door however, she suddenly felt her other hand being grabbed from behind by

three by three

Stuart. 'You're not going to do this alone,' he said as she turned back round.

'But you can't say here with me. You'll die.'

'Probably.'

'You need to jump. Don't throw your life away. You have things to live for. I don't.'

'A lot has happened this week, so much has happened that I don't think I'll ever understand it, but right now I finally understand why I trusted you and why I came back for you in that forest. I have you to live for, and you have me, but right now if it's going to end for one of us, then it can end for both of us.'

'But...'

'... This time, you need to trust me.'

Without a second thought, Cleo impulsively reached in to grab Stuart's head before pulling it closer and kissing him.

'What are they doing?' Marley asked Holly as they both continued to watch what was going on from the other helicopter.

'I'm not certain, but it looks as though they're kissing,' Holly replied.

'Yeah, it does. We should give that a go too.'

'Sorry?'

To Holly's surprise, even more impulsively than Cleo had with Stuart, Marley suddenly leant in towards her and began kissing her.

the end

By now Stuart and Cleo had broken off and taken their seats in the cockpit, but as they surveyed the dials and controls in front of them, they knew there was little hope of what they were planning ending well.

'Put this on,' Cleo said as she handed Stuart one of the headsets. 'We might be able to contact them over there,' she continued as he put on her own. 'Hello,' she then called out into the microphone.

They waited for a moment, but there was no response.

'They're probably on a different frequency to us,' Stuart said as he looked down at the small collection of dials and number between them.

'What do we try?'

'I think I've got an idea.'

Cleo watched as Stuart looked over at the other helicopter where Marley had just regained her professional composure. After a few seconds, he caught her eye, and she watched as he held up the headset and pointed at it.

'Holly I think they're trying to contact us,' Marley said as she climbed into the spare seat next to her.'

'Okay, I'll try all the channels,' Holly replied as she handed her a spare headset.

Stuart and Cleo waited in silence until eventually, they heard a crackle that was then followed shortly afterwards by Marley's voice. 'Can I just start by saying,' she began sounding happier than ever. 'Both of you were bloody good with that,'

three *by* three

she continued.

'Thanks,' Cleo replied. 'But we couldn't have done anything if it wasn't for your aim.'

'I appreciate that, but it's just my job. Also, don't worry too much about Ivan managing to jump, I've got in touch with MI5, and while they won't ever let me forget I needed help, they're already on the ground looking for him.'

'I'm sorry we couldn't stop him getting away.'

'You both did the best you could, and you did that well. Right now though, the important thing is getting you both back on the ground.'

'We don't have much fuel left on this.'

'Do you have any more parachutes?'

'We have one.'

'Do you want us to try to throw you another one over?'

'No.'

'Are you gong to try share?'

'We're not jumping.'

'What do you mean you're not jumping?'

'We can't jump. If we leave this as it is then it'll just fall out of the sky.'

'You can't stay in it though. You'll both risking your own lives if you do that.

'I know, but that's what you do for people every day. I'm going...' She paused and looked over at Stuart. 'We're going to try and make sure that when it does crash, it crashes away

the end

from people.'

'You don't have to do this.'

'I know I don't. You're father never had to lose his life to save my father's, but he chose to. I might be about to lose mine, but that's always going to be better than hundreds being lost below us.'

A pregnant pause followed as Marley thought. 'Cleo, if this is the last time we ever speak,' she began. 'Know this. I admire you.'

'I think you're the first person who ever has.'

'I disagree. Maybe the second, but certainly not the first. The first is the person who's sat next to you.' Stuart smiled. 'And Stuart, know this,' Marley continued. 'I got to know Spencer well during my life, and I know how picky he could be. But I don't have any doubt that he'd have had no concerns about you dating his daughter.'

'Oh,' Stuart replied in surprise. 'I don't... we're not...'

'... I saw you both kissing.' She paused. 'Cleo.'

'Yes?' Cleo replied.

'Good luck with this.'

They continued to listen until their headsets fell silent.

'Are you ready?' Cleo asked as they then looked each other in the face.

'Yes. I'm ready,' Stuart replied.

'Marley, was she right? Were you the first?'

'Yes. But not today, not yesterday and not even last week.'

three *by* three

'When then?'

'Early one September morning when we were both eleven.'

'I think... I think I...'

'Oh, and one last thing,' came Marley's voice again. 'I'm sorry I couldn't help you both earlier on, both with this and with Zachary. I should've been there to make sure you were safe.'

'You didn't need to be there,' Stuart replied. 'I had Cleo to make sure I was safe.'

Their headsets fell silent again.

'Did you know she's my sister?' Cleo asked with a smile.

Silence followed as the looked each other in the face again. 'So,' Stuart eventually said. 'Do you have any idea how to fly this thing?'

'No. But I think I'm about to learn.'

An alarm began to ring out as Cleo reached forwards and pressed a button to disable the autopilot. Within seconds they also felt a sudden drop in height, but, as Cleo quickly began to understand the controls, she was able to just about keep them at a constant altitude.

'I don't know exactly how much fuel is left,' she said. 'I'm just going to try land it anywhere I can. Look out for a large open space.'

'How about Kensington Gardens?' Stuart suggested as he looked out below them. 'It's only a couple of miles away.'

'Which direction?'

the end

'West.'

'Okay. Let's try for that. Kensington Gardens sounds like a good idea. I saw a picture of it once. It looked nice.'

Although she was far from confident with the controls, Cleo did her best to swing the helicopter around to face west. As she began to straighten up however, they lost more height and she was able to feel a definite drop in power.

'I don't think we'll be able to make Kensington.'

Stuart looked back out to find another place to land before suddenly he spotted a small grassy area that bordered the river. 'Over there,' he said pointing towards it. 'We should be able to make that.'

'Okay.'

Somewhat reluctantly, Cleo let the helicopter lose yet more height until they were only a hundred metres from the ground, but, as she lined up to aim for where Stuart had been pointing, she felt another, and this time even more noticeable, drop in power.

'I don't think we'll make it there either,' she said with worry as she did her best to keep control. Desperately she began looking around to find another place to land, but before she found somewhere, the entire cockpit fell into a deathly silence as the blades above them stopped turning.

With neither of them able to think of anything to say, they instead reached out and grabbed each other hands as the began falling at an increasing speed helplessly towards the

three *by* three

ground, before seconds later, there was a sudden hard impact, and then, nothing.

chapter fourteen
finally happy

Suddenly from nothing, there was a bright white light, but Cleo wasn't sure where it was coming from.

Slowly she opened her eyes and looked up at the ceiling above her. She was lying in a hospital bed, although she wasn't sure in which hospital, or how she'd got there.

'Well that's taken you a while,' she heard a voice say, although she felt too dazed to work out whose voice it was.

Gently she pushed herself up and looked around the room. Marley was sat on a chair at the bottom of her bed, smiling up at her. Cleo noticed she seemed to be dressed much more formal than usual.

'You've been out for over a week,' Marley continued. 'You managed to pick up some pretty nasty injuries.'

Cleo felt confused. She'd no idea what Marley was talking

three *by* three

about until suddenly she began to regain her senses and feel pain in almost every single part of her body. She looked down at her arm, but instead of seeing skin she saw a solid cast that was being held by a sling around her neck.

'It might be best if you didn't try to move too much.' Marley continued. 'Not until you've had a bit more time to recover anyway.'

'What happened?' Cleo asked, still feeling dazed.

'You crashed into a large tree.'

'I don't... I can't remember any of it.'

'I'd be surprised if you could, it wasn't a soft landing. If I'm telling you the truth, you're lucky to have woken up at all.'

Cleo looked around the room and noticed they were the only ones there. Suddenly her thoughts then turned to Stuart. He'd been sat next to her, the last thing she could remember seeing was his face. 'Where's Stuart?' she asked. 'He's not here too is he? He didn't die?'

Marley smiled at her. 'He's alive. You don't need to worry about that. He came round a few days ago, but he'll probably still be stuck in a wheelchair for a few more weeks though.'

'Where is he?'

'He's got his own room on another ward.'

'Am I able to see him?'

'Of course. I've no doubt you'll both have a lot to talk about, but wait until later, I need to talk to you right now.'

'What about?'

finally happy

'The future, more specifically… your future.'

'Oh… Well, I've not really had time to think about it,' Cleo said taken aback. 'Not yet anyway.'

'Of course you haven't, but still, I'm not someone who likes to waste time when there's no need to, and you clearly have some skills that could be put to good use.'

'I don't understand what you mean?'

'For someone who's never flown a helicopter before, you did a good job.'

'But I crashed it?'

'Well yes, that's true, and I highly doubt anyone will ever have the chance to fly that particular helicopter again in the future.' She paused and then smiled. 'But what's important is why you crashed it. You crashed it by choice. It'd have been much easier for you to have jumped out before it ran out of fuel…'

'… But people would've died when it fell out the sky,' Cleo interrupted.

'Exactly. You chose to stay and risk your own life to save others, and that makes you the sort of person we need.'

'Need?'

'As I believe Stuart would put it, more than a little has happened in less than a lot of time over the past few weeks. One of those things is the loss of my former colleague, Zachary, and his job is one that does now need to be filled by someone, only if you're interested of course?'

241

three *by* three

'But surely I'm in not fit state? I might never be.'

'I've been assured by your doctors that while it may take a few months, you'll make a full recovery. Until then the job can be held for you, after all, there's not much to do other than piles of paperwork at the moment anyway.'

'What about Stuart?'

'I've already spoken to him about it, and there's a job available for him too, my old one.'

'But you're not resigning, are you? You can't.'

'No I'm not resigning, but.' Marley paused, she knew she was about to bring up a difficult subject. 'Your father, it's very unfortunate that he's gone, but the fact is that he's left a role that needs to be filled, and I've been asked to fill it.'

Cleo smiled at her. 'I'm sure you'll be good at it.'

'He'd have been proud of you. I hope you know that. He'd have wanted you to.'

'I think he'd have been proud of you too.' Cleo stopped and thought for a moment. 'I'm sorry that you lost him as well.'

'It's hard, but I know it's harder for you. You weren't even given a chance to get to know him. Life doesn't always go the way we wish it could, all we can do is try to make the most of it and not let our thoughts linger too much on what's already happened. That's what my mother said to me after my father died. She always told me to remember that time spent missing those we no longer have takes time away from getting to know those we still do.' Marley stood up and walked over to the

finally happy

small table next to Cleo's bed that was topped with flowers and cards. 'Speaking of which,' she continued as she handed Cleo a small box of chocolates. 'A get well soon present from Stuart. I know they look small, but he wanted me to make sure you knew just how hard it was for him to get them. He's not in the best state to walk at the moment, and I don't think I've ever seen anyone quite so bad with crutches.'

Cleo couldn't help but laugh to herself.

'He really cares about you,' Marley continued. 'I've met men... it's the reason I'm not with one. But if Stuart didn't care then he wouldn't have stayed with you and risked his own life too.'

'Is all of this from him?' Cleo asked as she surveyed the table.

'No, not all of it.'

'Who's it from then? There're not that many people who know or care who I am.'

'You'd be surprised. Some of it's from people I work with and me.' Marley reached over to hand Cleo one of the cards. 'And then there's also this one.'

'Who's it from?'

'Open it.'

three *by* three

'It's from my mother?' Cleo asked as she looked back up at Marley.

'She's been to see you quite a few times.'

'She was at the funeral, wasn't she? My father's funeral, I saw her there. I thought you didn't know where she lived?'

'We've always known. Your father cared about her, he always did, and even if he'd never have admitted it, he liked to keep an eye on her and make sure she was always safe. He even got her out of the occasional speeding ticket without her knowing too.'

'Why didn't you tell me that before? You said she was his secretary at the funeral.'

'I did what I thought was best that day. I know I probably got it wrong and I apologise. You'd just said goodbye to your father and I thought it best if you weren't forced to go through any more emotions that day.'

Cleo looked down and read the card again.

'Anyway,' Marley said in a successful attempt to change the

finally happy

subject. 'I hope you don't mind me being rude, but there's somewhere else I need to be soon.'

'No, it's okay,' Cleo replied. 'I should probably rest.'

'Before I go though, I don't suppose you'd be able to help me out?'

'What with?'

'Would you mind if I took a bunch of your flowers with me?' Marley asked as she gestured towards the table.

'You can take them, but what do you need them for?'

'I'm about to have a meeting with the head of MI6, and they're not particularly happy with us at the moment.'

'Why not?'

'You know I just said you crashed into a large tree?'

'Yes?'

'Well it was their large tree. You crashed into their back garden.'

'Oh… I'm sorry.'

'No need to be sorry. If it were up to me, you'd receive an award for having an aim like that.' Marley smiled and picked up a bunch of flowers before turning to leave the room.

'There is one thing,' Cleo called after her.

Marley stopped and turned back round. 'Yes?'

'What happened to James and Ivan? Were they found?'

'Yes, they both were. James is fine. He landed in Kensington Gardens, a pretty perfect landing actually. As for Ivan, I doubt you'll ever see him again. His parachute didn't open.'

three *by* three

'Oh.'

'I do now keep getting angry phone calls from a woman who's not too happy about him landing in her garden though.'

Cleo laughed.

'I don't understand what she's complaining about,' Marley continued. 'She wasn't the one who had to clear the mess up.'

'Did you apologise to her?'

'I haven't got round to it yet.' There was a pause before Marley looked back over at the table. 'Would you mind if I took another…'

'… Take them.'

'Thanks,' Marley replied as she grabbed another bunch of flowers. 'I'll let Stuart know you've come round on my way out.'

'Thanks.'

Cleo watched as Marley left the room before then turning her attention back to the card from her mother. As she read it a third time, she reached around her neck with her non-injured arm and found she was still wearing the necklace from her father.

With the card in one hand and the necklace in the other, she then fell back and let her head rest on the soft pillow behind. Her final thought before she fell asleep was that even though her life was far from perfect, she was, for the first time she could remember, happy.

Lightning Source UK Ltd.
Milton Keynes UK
UKOW02f2116111216
289689UK00001B/6/P